THOROUGHBRED

ULTIMATE RISK

CREATED BY
JOANNA CAMPBELL

WRITTEN BY
MARY NEWHALL ANDERSEN

HarperEntertainment
An Imprint of HarperCollinsPublishers

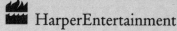
HarperEntertainment

An Imprint of HarperCollinsPublishers
10 East 53rd Street, New York, NY 10022-5299

 Produced by 17th Street Productions, Inc.

HarperCollins books are available at special quantity discounts for bulk purchases for sales promotions, premiums, or fund-raising. For information, please call or write: Special Markets Department, HarperCollins Publishers, 10 East 53rd Street, New York, NY 10022-5299. Telephone: (212) 207-7528. Fax: (212) 207-7222.

ISBN 0-06-106634-6

HarperCollins®, 📖 ®, and HarperEntertainment™ are trademarks of HarperCollins Publishers Inc.

Cover art © 2000 by 17th Street Productions, Inc.

First printing: April 2000

Printed in the United States of America

Visit HarperEntertainment on the World Wide Web at
www.harpercollins.com

❖ 10 9 8 7 6 5 4 3 2 1

*For Cecily, who deserves a lot of credit,
with special thanks to my fellow horse
and book lover, Margaret L.*

Ultimate
Risk

"IF YOU'RE DONE WITH THAT HOOF PICK, CAN I USE IT?" sixteen-year-old Christina Reese asked. She looked over the two-year-old chestnut Thoroughbred colt's back to where her cousin, Melanie Graham, was grooming another chestnut colt.

"Come and get it," Melanie said, setting Rascal's hoof down and holding out the hoof pick. Melanie's hair tie had slipped, freeing wisps of pale blond hair that framed her face, and she swiped at a few strands with the back of her hand.

Christina reached up to tighten the band that held her own long red-brown hair in a ponytail at the nape of her neck. Wonder's Star stood quietly while Christina ducked under his neck to reach for the pick.

Even though it was late summer, the early morning air had a cool edge to it. Like Christina, Melanie was wearing a zippered sweatshirt while she prepared Rascal for his morning workout at the Turfway Park racetrack in Florence, Kentucky.

It was barely five o'clock in the morning, but the two girls had been working on the track's backside for almost an hour, taking care of their horses and helping around the shedrow, the long row of stalls where the Thoroughbreds were housed during racing season.

Rascal struck at the ground and snorted, tugging at the crossties. Christina laughed. "I think he's telling you he's ready to go now!"

Around them, the furious activity of the backside had both colts alert and excited. Handlers were leading energetic colts and fillies toward the track, where trainers and exercise riders were waiting for them. Other horses were being groomed, while still others paced in their stalls, waiting to be fed. From another shedrow, the sound of a horse kicking its stall wall echoed around the backside. A groom hurried in the direction of the noise.

Christina turned to Star, who angled his head to look at her, then arched his neck and whinnied loudly, his entire body shaking with the effort. "I guess Star's ready, too," she said with a grin. Christina was sure anyone who saw Star had to feel the same admiration for him that she did. With powerful muscles rippling under his sleek, copper-colored coat, and bright, intelligent eyes set wide apart in a finely formed head, the colt was magnificent.

"He looks great," Melanie said from behind her.

"He's absolutely gorgeous," Christina said, giving Star an affectionate pat before she began cleaning his hooves.

"Rascal isn't too bad, either, you know," Melanie said as she shifted her exercise saddle on the colt's back. "Are you, boy?" Rascal pawed the ground again, his hindquarters dancing a little as she adjusted the girth.

Christina cast a glance at the other colt from over her shoulder. "Rascal does looks fantastic," she said, then returned her attention to Star. Although both colts had been bred at Whitebrook Farm, the breeding and training farm owned by Christina's parents, for Christina there would never be another horse as special as Star.

When her mother, Ashleigh Griffen, had decided to breed her Derby-winning mare, Ashleigh's Wonder, one last time, Ashleigh and Christina's father, Mike Reese, had decided on Jazzman, Mike's best stallion, as a sire.

But Wonder had developed complications and died after giving birth to Star, and Ashleigh had been devastated, blaming Star for Wonder's death. Her mother couldn't stand to look after the sickly orphaned foal herself, so Christina had stepped in to take care of him, raising Star by hand during his first year.

"Hurry up and get Star saddled. The track's going to start crowding up soon," Melanie said, drawing Christina's attention back to the present.

Christina nodded, picking up a saddle pad. "We'll be right behind you."

Melanie led the Rascal away while Christina adjusted her exercise saddle on Star's tall back. He twisted his neck, looking back at her, and Christina smiled at his eager expression. "Just a minute, boy," she said fondly, fastening the girth. "I know you want to get going, too."

When she lifted his bridle into place, Star practically grabbed the snaffle bit from her palm, shoving his nose into the headstall. "You're really ready to work, aren't you?" She fastened the throatlatch and led the excited colt away from Whitebrook's stabling area. Star pranced beside her, his ears pricked forward and his nostrils flared, as they approached the busy track.

By the time they reached the rail several horses

were already being worked on the oval. The morning mist had begun to lift, and the late summer sun was starting to warm the air. Christina spotted Melanie and Rascal trotting counterclockwise along the outside rail behind two other horses. A jockey was galloping his horse clockwise at the inside rail, and Star tossed his head, tugging at the reins as the running horse thundered by.

"Ready to go?"

At the sound of her mother's voice, Christina glanced over her shoulder. Ashleigh Griffen was dressed in worn jeans and a baggy sweatshirt, a Whitebrook Farm baseball cap covering her long brown hair. A stopwatch dangled from a cord around her neck, and she gripped a clipboard in one hand. To Christina, her petite mother looked more like a high-school girl than the well-respected jockey and horse trainer she was.

"We're ready," Christina said as Star danced around, his eyes fixed on the track.

"He looks excellent, Chris," Ashleigh said, giving Star's glistening neck a pat. She let her gaze linger on the colt's muscled form for a moment, then turned her attention to Christina again. "He's had a good rest since he ran in the Laurel Stakes. It's time to schedule another race for Star."

"Did you have a particular one in mind?" Christina asked. Her mother, along with Ian McLean, White-brook's head trainer, was constantly researching races, looking for the best ones to run the farm's horses in.

Ashleigh nodded. "The Breeder's Futurity," she said.

"But that's less than two weeks away, Mom!" Christina stared at her mother. The Futurity was a significant race for two-year-olds. The horses that stood out in races such as the Futurity went on to be the next year's Derby contenders. "Are you sure he's ready?"

Ashleigh nodded firmly. "Ian and I both agree that Star's ready for another challenge. The Futurity will have some big-time competition, but Star's best times are right up there." Christina had a great deal of respect for Whitebrook's head trainer. If Ian didn't think Star was up to handling the Futurity, he never would have suggested it.

"Will I be his jockey?" Christina asked in a small voice.

"Of course," Ashleigh said with a confident smile. "I know the two of you can handle it."

Christina grimaced slightly. Even though Ashleigh had ridden Star to a win the month before, she still insisted he ran his best for Christina. And Christina and Star had proven her right by putting in an even

6

faster time in the Laurel Stakes. As far as Ashleigh was concerned, Star was a one-jockey horse.

But in a race such as the Futurity, the best jockeys would be competing—jockeys with years of experience, compared to her few months as an apprentice jockey. Christina knew Star could run the race well enough, but she hoped she would be able to hold her own against seasoned riders.

Ashleigh patted Star's shoulder. "Come on, let's get you both onto the track."

Christina collected Star's reins and let her mother give her a leg up onto Star's back. Ashleigh held Star's head, and Christina reached down to catch her stirrups as she settled onto the lightweight saddle.

She was tall for a jockey, and with her feet wedged into the supershort stirrups, her calves almost touched the backs of her thighs. Fortunately she was slender and small-boned, so she didn't have any trouble maintaining a good racing weight.

"Keep him to an easy two-mile jog today," Ashleigh said, holding Star's bridle with one hand and resting her free hand on Christina's knee. Star tossed his head as a horse galloped by. "Then give him a short gallop, just to blow him out a bit. The day after tomorrow we'll breeze him." Christina knew that all those great times she and Star had gotten on the practice track at home didn't count toward the track records. They needed a few good times clocked by Turfway's official timer to boost their reputation.

Christina nodded. Ashleigh released the colt, stepping back as Christina guided him onto the track. Melanie steered Rascal past the gap as Star headed along the outside rail.

As Melanie and Rascal fell into step beside them, Star fought Christina for a moment, trying to pick up the pace. "This is just an exercise day, silly," Christina said softly, stroking his arched neck. Star strained at the bit for a second longer, then seemed to understand. He settled down, relaxing his neck and moving along the track in an extended trot.

Melanie stayed beside them, keeping her eyes forward as Rascal flicked his ears and tried to snatch the reins away from her. Christina could see Melanie's entire body tense as her cousin yanked fiercely on the reins. But even when Rascal slowed, Melanie's jaw remained set. Christina looked on worriedly as Rascal picked up on Melanie's obvious stress. The colt scampered a little, as though he thought he could run away from Melanie's tension.

"Mel, are you okay?"

Melanie nodded stiffly. "He's just acting up a little," she said, easing up on the reins. In response, Rascal dropped his head and continued on at a steady trot.

Christina frowned. Although Rascal's antics weren't any worse than usual, Melanie's reaction had seemed extreme. But as they continued along the rail Melanie seemed to relax. Christina wondered if she was reading too much into the moment.

"Guess what?" she said as they moved into the first turn. "Mom is putting Star in the Breeder's Futurity."

"Great," Melanie said, her eyes fixed on the view from between Rascal's ears. "That'll be an exciting race."

"I hope I can get some other trainers to let me ride before then," Christina went on. "I want to get in as many races as I can. And as many wins."

Melanie nodded, still not letting her attention stray from Rascal. "What about Phil Oberman?" she asked. "He had plenty of claimers for you to ride last month at Ellis Park."

Christina shook her head. "I checked," she said. "Phil didn't bring any horses to Turfway. But he'll be running some horses at Keeneland for the fall meet. I'm sure I can pick up some rides from him there."

Phil was young and still working his way up the training ranks. He had been the first trainer, besides her mother, to let Christina race his horses. She had learned a lot working with Phil, and she had done well, too, winning on horses that even Phil hadn't thought had it in them. Riding claimers like Phil's was a good way to earn enough wins to get her full jockey's license, but the purses were small. The money was barely enough to pay for her half of the motel room she and Melanie were sharing for the first two weeks of Turfway's short season, and for the fast-food meals they had to eat while living away from home.

What Christina wanted was the chance to ride for a bigger stable and a more prestigious trainer. If she could win some large purses, she might eventually have enough money to buy Townsend Acres' half of Wonder's Star.

If all of the Townsends were like Clay Townsend, who had given her mother half ownership in Ashleigh's Wonder years before Christina had been born, or like Parker Townsend, Clay's handsome grandson, sharing ownership of Star with them wouldn't be a problem. But Parker's father, Brad, oversaw Townsend Acres, and Brad was the most self-centered, arrogant person Christina had ever met. Brad's head trainer, Ralph Dunkirk, had nearly ruined Star the previous year, while he was stabled at Townsend Acres, and Christina could never forgive Brad, or Ralph, for the rough treatment the colt had received there.

The only way Star could ever be totally safe from

Brad's interference was for her to buy the Townsends' interest in the colt—not that the Townsends were interested in selling. Christina hated to put a price on Star, because as far as she was concerned, he was priceless, but she figured if she offered enough money, Brad wouldn't be able to resist. She didn't want to ask her parents for help, so saving up was a long, slow process.

Christina gave the colt's neck another pat, letting her hand rest there for a moment, feeling the play of muscles under his warm, smooth coat.

Just then a dark brown colt came thundering toward them in the opposite direction, hugging the inside rail of the track. A petite woman was perched lightly on the horse's shoulders, and Christina turned her head to watch the horse and rider finish their breeze.

"That was Vicky Frontiere, wasn't it?" she asked. Vicky, a friend of Ashleigh's, had helped Christina get her apprentice license last spring.

Melanie nodded. "She was on that Pam Mahony colt, Decisive Moment," she said, her voice sounding a little flat.

"I thought *you* were going to work Dee for Pam," Christina said, surprised.

Melanie shrugged, slowing Rascal as they neared

the gap. "I was," she said. "But I changed my mind."

"You what?" Christina gaped at Melanie, but her cousin brought Rascal to a stop and jumped off the colt without responding. Christina held Star to a trot, moving away from Melanie and Rascal. She had to force herself to pay attention to the activity on the track, but she was puzzled by Melanie's odd behavior. Dee was an amazing horse. Why would Melanie have decided not to ride him?

When they reached the end of the straight stretch, Christina turned Star and moved to the inside rail, preparing for his short gallop before she took him off the track.

Just as she moved forward in the saddle, cueing Star to speed up, a jockey on a sturdy bay colt flew past them on the inside, startling Christina. She recognized the jockey, Steve Quinn, but she'd never seen the horse before.

Christina was almost pleased to see the bay colt giving Steve some trouble. She didn't care for Steve, who had recently come to Kentucky from New York, where he'd been riding at Belmont. As far as Christina was concerned, the other jockey was a little too full of himself, and when he wasn't bragging about his own experiences, he was usually running someone else down.

As the bay colt moved away from them, Star jerked his head and picked up his speed. Christina struggled to slow him. Star hated to be passed, and Christina didn't blame him, but just then they had a job to do, and it wasn't to outrun Steve Quinn and his unruly mount.

She sat back and half-halted in an attempt to slow Star, but the bay suddenly snapped his head up and stopped abruptly, right in Star's path. Steve reached back with his whip and smacked the colt on the rump, trying to drive the horse forward. But as he lunged ahead, the colt brought his nose down between his front legs and threw his rump into the air, nearly dislodging Steve with a massive buck.

Star was bearing down swiftly on the bucking colt, and Christina hauled on the reins, trying to turn him. But even as Star started to go wide, the bay threw his head up and then reared, thrashing at the sky with flailing hooves. But still the jockey clung to his back. The enraged colt spun around on his hind legs, losing his balance. Finally he went over backward, spilling his rider on the track right in front of Star, who had barely checked his gallop.

2

CHRISTINA'S HEART SLAMMED INTO HER THROAT. THEY were almost on top of the other horse!

The muscular bay was still for the moment, but at any second he would try to scramble to his feet. Instinctively Christina moved into a two-point jumping position, collecting Star's reins and tangling her fingers in his mane. She balanced precariously over Star's shoulders as he sprang into the air.

The bay began to roll over, and for a terrifying instant Christina thought Star was going to catch the other horse with his hooves. But even as she braced herself for the impact, Star was landing safely on the other side of the fallen horse and rider.

A rush of relief coursed through Christina. Her

hands trembled as she fumbled with the reins, trying to stop Star. The colt pranced sideways along the track, fighting to keep going. When he finally came to a halt, Christina jumped from his back.

Ashleigh raced onto the track, skidding to a stop beside Star.

"His legs," Christina gasped, her heart thundering in her chest, her own legs shaking so badly she could barely stand. "Get the vet to check his legs, Mom." From the corner of her eye she could see the red light flashing at the top of the pole in the infield, signaling trouble on the track.

Ashleigh nodded grimly. "She's on her way," she said, dropping to her knees beside Star.

"He's never jumped like that," Christina said, almost in tears. "What if he's hurt himself?" Just the thought of Star hurt made a lump form in her throat, and she gulped back a sob.

"I think he's okay, Chris," her mother said in a reassuring voice as she ran her hands down both his front legs. The vet's little pickup pulled onto the track, and Ashleigh rose as the woman climbed from her truck, the track van stopping behind her.

The other horses that had been working had been taken off the track as soon as the red light had come on. Now trainers and riders clustered at the rail, waiting for the vet to do her job so they could get back to work.

The vet flashed a look at Christina. "Nice steeple-chasing," she said. "You obviously know how to handle a jumping horse. It's too bad you couldn't have just gone around."

Christina pressed her lips together. As if she had purposely jumped Star! But the vet turned away, focusing her attention on Star while Christina stroked his neck to keep him quiet.

"He looks okay," the vet said while she wrapped both Star's legs in support bandages. She rose and smiled at Christina. "Your jumping skill, combined with pure luck, probably prevented any injury," she said. "But you should have X rays done, just to be certain his joints are okay." She pressed her toe against the track's surface "Fortunately the ground is soft here, so his landing was cushioned."

"I'll take him over to the track clinic for his X rays," Ashleigh said, taking Star's reins from Christina. "You go take a nice hot shower and change," she ordered, gently squeezing Christina's shaking hand.

"I'll go with you," Christina started to protest, but Ashleigh shook her head.

"After you shower, meet me at the barn. I'll take good care of Star, okay?"

Christina didn't argue, and stood watching as her

mother lead the colt away. She glanced behind her to see the vet striding toward the other horse. The colt was on his feet, his ears pinned as he snapped at the stocky man holding his bridle. She couldn't see the handler's face, but the man looked vaguely familiar to Christina. He was dressed like a trainer, in khaki slacks and a tweed jacket, and was paying little attention to the angry colt, who pranced and yanked against the grip on his headstall. In spite of his wild behavior, the colt was magnificent-looking—thickset, with long legs, massive shoulders and hindquarters, and bright, intelligent eyes. He was more like locomotive than a sports car and not as elegant as Star, but with that kind of conformation, he could definitely run.

The trainer's attention was locked on Steve Quinn, his eyes blazing. The jockey stood in front of the trainer with his arms folded across his chest, an angry scowl on his face.

"If you can't handle something as simple as exercising the colt, how do you plan to race him?" the trainer yelled. "You could have ruined two good horses out there."

"It was that exercise rider's fault," Steve said, jerking his chin at Christina. "She wasn't paying any attention. Didn't you see? She turned her horse right in front of us. That's what set Gratis off. What a space case."

Christina went rigid. She couldn't believe Steve was blaming her! The bay colt hadn't been anywhere near them until he stopped right in their path!

"You've got to watch out for those inept little wannabes," the trainer growled. "They can barely ride. You should know that by now."

Christina clenched her fists and ground her teeth. She was no inept little wannabe jockey. She took a step toward the trainer, who still had his back to her.

"If you plan to keep riding for me, you'd better get your act together," the man said loudly, then dismissed Steve with a brusque wave of his hand. Christina could see Steve bristle and start to open his mouth, then clamp it shut and walk away as the trainer turned to the vet, who was running her hands over the big bay's white-stockinged leg.

Christina did a double take when she recognized the weathered features under the brim of the trainer's battered gray fedora. The man holding the ill-mannered colt was none other than Vince Jones, the most renowned trainer in Kentucky. And now, thanks to Steve Quinn, he thought she was a careless rider.

Steve stormed past her, casting a contemptuous look in her direction. "Nice going, hotshot," he said.

"If you hadn't cut us off, my colt would have been fine."

Christina's jaw dropped, but before she could respond, Steve was off the track and hurrying toward the locker room. She glared at his retreating back.

The vet walked by, heading for her truck.

"Is the bay colt okay?" Christina asked as the vet passed her.

"Crazy as it seems, he's fine," the vet said, frowning. "I'm no trainer, but I don't think that colt has the mind to be on the track. We were fortunate there wasn't a lot of traffic out here this morning, and that your horse had the scope to jump over that mess. We're lucky I'm not putting both these horses down with broken legs. Mr. Jones should think twice before he puts anyone up on that horse." With that, Christina walked away.

Christina gazed back at the handsome bay who was yanking the lead shank out of Vince Jones's hand. What had she heard Steve call him? *Gratis . . . I wonder what that means*. The colt angled his head, looking in her direction, and Christina could see a keen intelligence in his eyes. The vet couldn't be right. This horse was smart, and judging from his powerful build, he was meant for speed. Steve just didn't know how to handle him.

She wondered how it would feel to win his trust, be

19

able to ride him on the track. But he was Vince Jones's horse, and Vince had a waiting list of riders who wanted to work for him. If he was having trouble getting riders to work the bay, though, it just might be her chance to show the famous trainer she was a capable jockey, not an inept bug.

"Mr. Jones?" She took a step toward the trainer, who glanced in her direction.

Just then a handler hurried onto the track. Vince Jones shoved the colt's reins into his hands. "Next time you wander off and leave me to do *your* job will be the last time!" he said sharply. Then he wheeled to face Christina.

"What did you want?" he asked abruptly, then glanced around, looking over her head as though she weren't even there.

Christina's question died in her throat. It probably wasn't the best time to ask him for a job. "Nothing," she murmured. "I'm glad your colt is okay."

"Right," he said, then glanced at his watch and hurried off the track.

The other horses and riders were coming back onto the track to resume their works, and Christina followed the bay colt off the track.

"Nice job," a familiar voice said.

Christina looked up to see Pam Mahony smiling at

her. She had exercise-ridden one of the trainer's fillies earlier in the week, and she liked how quiet and easygoing Pam always seemed to be around the horses.

"Thanks," Christina said. "That scared me to death."

"You handled it like a real professional," Pam said.

"Well, thanks for trying to make me feel better," Christina said. "But I don't think jumping over Gratis was the best way to get Vince Jones to notice me." She sighed, unbuckling her helmet as she walked along the rail with the trainer. "I'm just glad it wasn't me he was yelling at."

Pam chuckled. "Vince yells at everybody," she said. "He's the most irritable man in racing. But he's still the best trainer in the state."

Christina glanced down the track to where Vince Jones was standing, watching a gray filly breeze.

"Someday," she said, "I'd like to ride for him."

Pam followed her gaze to where Vince was holding a stopwatch, staring intently as the filly thundered along the inside rail.

"Be careful what you wish for," Pam said, laughing. "He's a hard man to work for. I should know—I was one of his assistant trainers."

"Really?" Christina asked in awe. "What was it like?"

"Well, you have to have a hide as thick as a rhinoceros's to work for Vince," she said. "He doesn't cut anyone any slack. But he's also one of the greatest teachers there is. And he gets great horses."

"Vicky Frontiere and Tommy Turner have both ridden for him," Christina said. Along with Vicky, Tommy had helped Christina test for her apprentice jockey's license, and both the jockeys had a few wild Vince Jones stories. Like the time he thought Tommy was getting lazy, so he made him work a horse blindfolded. But even if Vince was intimidating, Christina knew she could learn a lot from the gruff old trainer, if he would only give her a chance.

A galloping horse drew her attention back to the track. "I saw Vicky breezing Decisive Moment," she said, watching the rider slow his horse. "They looked great together. Will she be racing him for you?"

Pam shook her head. "I'm putting him in the Kentucky Cup," she said. "But Vicky is riding for June Fortig in the Cup." She frowned, looking Christina up and down. "How would you like to take him on the track for me?"

"Me?" Christina gaped at the trainer.

Pam nodded. "After watching you win the Laurel Stakes last month, I think you'd do well with Dee."

"But the Kentucky Cup!" Christina protested.

"That's a big race, Pam. Are you sure?"

"Honestly, Chris, you weren't my first choice," Pam said. "Your cousin, Melanie, does so well with the difficult horses, I offered Dee to her first, but she said she couldn't do it. So the ride is yours if you want it."

Christina hesitated. She still didn't understand why Melanie had turned Pam down. She hoped her taking the ride wouldn't bother Melanie.

"I'd love to," she said quickly. "And don't worry, we're going to win."

"Good for you," Pam said, smiling. "That'll be one more win for Dee's record, and one more toward losing your bug."

Apprentice jockeys needed forty-five winning rides and a year of experience in order to lose the "bug," the asterisk on the racing program that indicated apprentice status. Even thought Christina had won her fair share of races, she still needed another thirty successful rides. And although the licensing rules allowed her three years to earn those wins, she wanted get her full license before her first year was up. Secretly she hoped the track stewards would approve her license on the first anniversary of her first win.

"I have a couple of horses for you to work tomorrow morning if you're interested," Pam offered.

"I'll be here," Christina promised. "Thanks." She

headed for the track's backside, passing horses that were on their way to the track for their workouts. The morning works would continue until ten o'clock, when the grounds crew would begin grooming the course for the afternoon's races.

Christina walked into the veterinarians' barn, swinging her helmet by the chin strap. The woman at the clinic's front desk smiled in greeting.

"Your mom took your colt back to his stall," the woman told her. "He's fine."

Relieved, Christina hurried toward the lockers. She'd do as her mother said and take a long, hot shower before she went back to the stables. But as she neared the entrance to the jockey room, George Stewart, an older jockey who had been giving her a hard time about her bug status, strode out of the building. The dark-haired jockey still acted like a jerk, but she hadn't let his arrogance and rudeness get to her. She was gradually proving herself to most of the other jockeys, anyway. George didn't have the power to upset her anymore.

"Good luck today, George," Christina said, forcing herself to smile at him.

George stared at her, startled. "Thanks," he said stiffly. "Couldn't find any claimers to race today, huh?"

Christina felt her jaw tighten, and she held her smile in place. "Nope," she said nonchalantly. "But if I were riding, I'd beat you."

George rolled his eyes. "Maybe in those little races you do so well at," he said. "But if you didn't have that chestnut colt to help you, you'd never win anything bigger than a third-rate claiming race."

"Don't be so sure." She lifted her chin. "I may just surprise you." She left him looking puzzled as she slipped through the door of the jockey room.

She wished she felt as confident as her words sounded, but she was afraid George was right. The claiming races were one thing, but without Star, against a field of top-rated horses and good jockeys, she didn't know how well she would do.

She hurried past the cluster of sofas and chairs where several jockeys had gathered. Most of them were dressed in sweatsuits, playing cards and talking as they waited for the races to begin.

She found Melanie standing in front of a mirror in the women's locker room, dragging a comb through her hair. Unhappy living in New York City, Melanie had come to Kentucky to stay with the Reeses four years before. She'd earned her apprentice license nearly a year earlier, and had been racing regularly ever since.

"Do you think I should dye my hair green?" Melanie said, eyeing Christina's reflection in the mirror.

"Then horses would probably think it was grass and try to eat it," Christina said with a grin.

Melanie wrinkled her nose. "Never mind, then," she said.

Christina sat down on a bench to pull off her boots. "Are you homesick for New York or something?" she asked. "Is that why you want to dye your hair?"

Ever since Melanie's father and stepmother had visited a few weeks earlier, she had been quieter and more withdrawn than usual.

"No, not really," Melanie said. "I wish I could spend more time with Dad and Susan, but I wouldn't trade Kentucky for New York, ever. I love it here."

"Good," Christina said as she peeled off her socks. Her gaze settled on the backs of her hands. She had been riding so much that her knuckles were developing calluses where they rubbed against the horses' necks. She massaged the rough skin lightly, then glanced up at Melanie. "How come you turned Pam down when she asked you to ride Dee in the Kentucky Cup?"

Melanie shrugged, then busied herself packing her hair dryer and exercise clothes into her duffel bag. "I just didn't feel up to riding him," she said.

"Are you sure?" Christina eyed Melanie closely. "Because she asked if I would ride him instead."

Melanie glanced up quickly, her eyes widening. She stiffened her shoulders, then nodded. "Great," she said with forced enthusiasm. "I hope you guys win."

Christina examined her cousin's profile. Melanie was definitely acting strange. What had happened to the feisty, opinionated, hilarious Mel? It was odd, too, that she didn't ask if Christina and Star were okay after what had happened that morning. She had to have heard about it by now.

"What's up, Mel? Is everything okay?" Christina demanded, frowning over at Melanie. "Are you worried about today's race?" Melanie was scheduled to ride Mischief Maker, one of Whitebrook's four-year-old mares, in a stakes race.

Melanie slowly zipped her bag shut. "Nah, I'm not worried at all," she said casually. "Missy and I get along great."

Christina sighed. Maybe it wasn't just her parents' visit but the bad spill her cousin had taken while they were there that was affecting Melanie's attitude. The bruises had quickly faded, but looking back, Christina realized Melanie had been very careful about which horses she rode since her fall. And when she raced, she was cautious to the point of missing opportunities that might have led to wins. Christina stared down at her bare feet and said nothing. She wished Melanie would confide in her.

"Are you going to take a shower or just sit there and stare at those ugly, smelly feet of yours?"

Christina looked up, relieved to hear some liveliness in Melanie's voice.

"Let's make the rounds of the backside when I'm done," Christina said, rising and peeling off her perspiration-soaked T-shirt. "We both need to hustle some rides for next weekend, and with school starting the week after that, we're not going to have much time. I think we should let the trainers know we'll be around to work on the weekends." She grabbed a towel from a stack at the end of the row of lockers. "It'll be great when Keeneland reopens next month. I'm tired of staying in that motel room."

Since Turfway Park was eighty miles from the Reeses' home in Lexington, Christina and Melanie were staying in a motel near the racetrack. "I miss my own bed," Christina said.

"You miss Parker, you mean," Melanie said in a teasing voice.

"That too," Christina said with a grin, thinking of her boyfriend, Parker Townsend. "Don't you miss

28

Kevin a little, too?" Since moving to Whitebrook, Melanie had been good friends with Ian McLean's son, Kevin, and recently they had started dating.

Melanie nodded. "A little," she admitted.

"It'll be nice when one of us finally gets our driver's license," Christina said. "Then we can come and go when we need to."

Melanie nodded. "No kidding. I'm sure your mom and dad will be happy not to have to haul us around, too."

Christina took a step toward the showers, then stopped. "You'll be great on Missy today, Mel."

At the mention of the race, Melanie's smile froze. "I hope so," she said.

"I know so," Christina replied. "Hold on. I'll be ready to go in a minute."

Melanie zipped her bag shut and headed for the door. "I'll see you in the jockey room."

Christina step into shower and let the hot water pummel her sore, tired muscles, washing away the difficulties of the morning. At least Melanie hadn't seemed mad that Christina would be riding Dee in his next race. But her cousin didn't seem very happy, either.

When Christina finished dressing, she hurried back to the jockey room to find Melanie. She was eager to start visiting the trainers who had horses stabled at Turfway for the month-long racing season. The money she and Melanie made exercise-riding helped cover their living expenses at the track, and the number and sheer variety of mounts gave them the chance to show the trainers how well they could handle different horses.

Just outside the locker room she stopped short, staring across the jockey room. Melanie was sitting in a chair, gazing up at Steve Quinn, who was leaning over her and talking quietly.

Christina felt her jaw tighten. What could Melanie possibly have to say to that jerk? But when Steve leaned close and spoke in her ear, Melanie flung her head back and laughed loudly.

Christina exhaled and pinched her mouth shut, waiting for Melanie to notice her. When they continued to ignore her, Christina started across the room.

Steve and Melanie glanced up at the same time. As she drew near, Steve whispered something to Melanie, then turned and stalked off. Christina glared at his back.

"Did Mr. Charm dazzle you with his great personality?" she asked as Melanie rose.

"Steve is perfectly nice," Melanie said defensively

as they headed for the door. "It's nice to talk with someone who knows some of the same places I used to go to in New York."

Christina felt her jaw tighten. "Did he tell you about this morning on the track?" she asked, remembering how Steve had blamed her for his wreck. "He could have injured Star!"

Melanie glanced at Christina. "I wasn't going to say anything, Chris, but Steve told me you turned Star right in front of him and cut his colt off. Steve managed to get the colt away from you and Star before he threw himself over backward. I know you didn't mean to, but *you* caused the accident."

A wave of disbelief surged over Christina. "And you believe him?"

Christina could see Melanie's answer in her expression. She sucked in a deep breath, trying to remember that Steve, with his stories of New York City and his charm and good looks, probably made Melanie feel pretty good. But Christina's sense of betrayal was overwhelming.

"He's a good jockey, Chris." Melanie gave her a quick look. "He's been riding for years. He wouldn't have done something so careless." Melanie started walking faster, and Christina hurried to keep up.

"I did not cut him off," Christina exclaimed. "I

can't believe you want to be friends with him. Steve's nothing but a jerk!"

"You don't need to baby-sit me, Chris," Melanie snapped. "And I can pick my own friends!"

Christina stopped, gaping at her cousin's back as Melanie hurried toward the shedrows.

3

CHRISTINA WATCHED MELANIE HURRY AWAY. HER COUSIN had been too quick to take Steve's word about what happened, but getting into a fight with Melanie wasn't going to help anything. She caught up with Melanie, falling into step beside her.

"I'm sorry, Mel. I didn't mean to upset you," she said as they walked side by side along a row of stalls. Horses hung their heads over some of the half doors, watching the activity around them. A groom pushed a wheelbarrow of soiled bedding down the aisle, hurrying to finish his work before the horses were returned to their stalls after working on the track. "I wasn't trying to tell you what to do."

Melanie glanced at her but kept walking. "I'm

sorry I snapped at you," she said. "I guess I *am* a little stressed about this afternoon. My last few races haven't exactly been stunning."

"You'll be fine," Christina said quickly. "You and Missy always do well together, and besides, you've almost won tons of times." Maybe riding the experienced racehorse would help Melanie's confidence on the track.

"Too many," Melanie said, frowning. "I'm getting tired of not coming in any better than second, race after race."

"I've heard of that happening to jockeys," Christina said. "Vicky calls it 'seconditis,' but I thought she was joking."

Melanie snorted. "Whatever she calls it, it's getting old really fast. She didn't happen to mention a cure for it, did she?"

"Sorry," Christina said. "I guess you just have to keep trying."

The shedrows were uncharacteristically quiet at the moment. Horses were eating after their morning works, or enjoying a bath at the wash racks. A few handlers and trainers sat in front of their stalls, talking idly, but for the most part, the track's backside had an almost sleepy quality.

When they came to the stables that housed Whitebrook's horses, Christina could see it was as peaceful in front of their stalls as it was everywhere else. Neither Maureen Mack, Whitebrook's assistant trainer, nor the two grooms, Dani and Joe, were in sight.

But as Christina and Melanie drew near the stalls, Christina heard a loud whinny. Star stuck his head over a stall door and flipped his nose in their direction. "There's my boy!" Christina said, hurrying to the stall. Star nudged her as she rubbed her hand over the gleaming white star on his forehead. The colt nickered softly, lipping her T-shirt.

"Hey, greedy." She laughed, gently pushing his nose away. "I don't have any goodies for you right now. I'll bring you an apple later, okay?"

"He always gets so excited when you're around," Melanie said. "You're lucky to have him."

"I know," Christina agreed. "Star is the greatest horse in the world, aren't you, boy?" The colt wiggled his upper lip against the palm of her hand. Christina loved Star more than she had ever loved another horse. Of course, she still loved Sterling Dream, her old eventing horse, but she had been with Star since his birth and they had gone through a lot together.

"He adores you," Melanie said, dropping into a plastic chair someone had left by the stall door.

Christina leaned her head against Star's cheek, but

her eyes were on Melanie. Normally so buoyant, Melanie's behavior was uncharacteristically tight-lipped and jumpy. "Why can't you tell me what's wrong?" Christina asked.

Melanie shrugged, staring at the ground. "It's nothing, really," she said. "I just need to win a race again, to know I can do it. Then I'll be fine."

"Are you sure that's all?" Christina frowned down at her cousin.

Melanie looked up and gave her a firm nod. "I'm positive," she said, rising.

"Then I predict that you and Missy will win your stakes race and you'll get over your seconditis." Star began lipping at Christina's hair, and she absently rubbed his soft nose, breathing in his sweet, horsy fragrance.

Melanie gave her a confident grin. "Sounds good to me."

Star raised his head and curled his upper lip, making both girls laugh. "Either he's agreeing with us or he doesn't like the taste of my shampoo," Christina said, pulling her hair back.

"Chris, Melanie!" Christina glanced away from Star as Maureen approached the stabling area. Beside her, Dani Martens, one of Whitebrook's grooms, led Mischief Maker toward the stalls.

The filly was in her last season as a racehorse. Missy was wearing a blue-and-white sheet over her shiny chestnut coat, and her legs were wrapped from knee to fetlock. Bobbing her pretty head and skittering sideways when a leaf fluttered across the path, she hardly looked as though she was ready to end her racing career. But next spring Christina's parents planned to retire her for use as a broodmare at Whitebrook.

Melanie walked to Missy's side as Dani stopped in front of her stall. The filly arched her neck and pranced, tugging at the lead line.

"Are you ready to run, girl?" Melanie asked the horse, stroking her sleek neck. Missy calmed down a little, but still snorted and tugged at her lead line, eager to keep moving.

"She's definitely ready," Dani said, setting her bucket of grooming supplies down beside the stall wall.

"That little blowout work we gave her two days ago really got her on her toes," Maureen said. "She's going to come out of the gate running and stay out front the whole way."

"I hope so," Melanie replied, opening the stall door so Dani could put Missy away.

"We need to get going if we're going to try to pick up some new rides," Christina said, giving Star one last pat. "We only have an hour before weigh-in time." She dropped a kiss on Star's nose. "I'll be back to see you in a little while, boy."

Melanie headed for one shedrow, while Christina went in the opposite direction, walking past June Fortig's stalls. She had approached the trainer earlier in the summer about riding for her, but June hadn't needed a rider then.

"Hey, Reese!"

Christina turned as June came out of the stall she used as a combination storeroom and office.

"I haven't seen you since Ellis Park last month," June said, shoving her hands into the pockets of her worn jeans. "Congratulations, by the way, on the Laurel Stakes win. That was a great ride."

"Thanks," Christina said. "I think all the riding I did for Phil Oberman really helped me. He put me on a lot of difficult claimers."

June looked smug. "I was the one who told you to go see him, remember?"

"Of course I remember," Christina said.

"How would you like to exercise some horses for me?" June asked. "I pay ten dollars a ride for the good horses and fifteen for the difficult ones." She shot Christina a quick grin. "But all *my* horses are easy, you know."

"I'm sure," Christina said with a laugh. She agreed to exercise two of June's horses, then headed for the next barn, where a groom directed her to the stable office. By the time she ran into Melanie, Christina had finagled four claiming races for the next few days, a stakes race for the coming weekend, and three new horses to exercise. Pretty good for a bug.

"I got three claiming races and one more exercising job. That's it," Melanie said, looking disgusted.

"I heard Phil Oberman's dad is here. Maybe he needs a rider. Come on." Christina led the way toward the senior Oberman's stables, stopping abruptly when she rounded a corner.

They were at the end of Vince Jones's stabling area. Christina could see Tommy Turner standing with the famous trainer, the two men deep in conversation. She watched Vince nod seriously as Tommy gestured toward the stalls. She wondered how it would feel to have a trainer such as Vince Jones listen to her that way, instead of ignoring her as though she were some annoying kid.

"That man is scary," Melanie said in a soft voice. "I've never seen him talk normally to someone before. Usually he's yelling."

"I know," Christina whispered nervously. She stared at the burly trainer, who towered over Tommy.

Christina gaped as Vince laughed at something Tommy said. She grabbed Melanie's arm. "Did you see that?" she hissed. "He smiled!"

"I think he was just baring his teeth," Melanie said dryly.

Heartened by seeing an almost friendly side to the famous trainer, Christina squared her shoulders. "I'm going to offer to exercise-ride for him," she announced.

"Are you nuts?" Melanie gasped. "He'll probably just snap your head off."

"The worst thing he can do is say no," Christina countered, trying not to let the butterflies in her stomach take off.

"It's your funeral," Melanie replied, shaking her head. "I'm going back to the locker room. Then I need to weigh in."

"I'll see you at the track," Christina said.

Melanie walked away, and Christina headed down the shedrow.

"No way am I taking that bay colt onto the track, Vince," Tommy was saying as Christina got near enough to hear them. "I saw him in action this morning. That colt is a suicide ride, and I don't want it."

Vince shook his head and spat in the dirt. "He's fast," he said. "He's got more potential than any other colt I have. But he's mean and impossible. I don't blame you."

"You going to tell his owner to get rid of him?"

Vince frowned. "I've tried. But she's stubborn. Insists that colt is going to wake up one day and run like a champ. I want to believe her, I really do. But I'm losing faith, fast."

Christina realized they were talking about the colt Steve had ridden earlier. She leaned against a stall wall, waiting for them to finish their conversation so she could approach the trainer. Finally Tommy stepped away.

"I'll see you at the viewing paddock before the second race," she heard Vince say as the jockey walked off.

But before Christina could take a step toward him, Vince turned and strode down the aisle at a furious clip. She considered hurrying after him but decided against it. She was sure chasing him along the shedrow would only annoy him.

Christina slumped against the barn wall, trying to figure out what to do next. The morning works had ended, and horses were being led back to their stalls. She noticed a groom leading an elegant black filly along the aisle, her coat covered in a purple-and-green cooling sheet. The groom stopped her a few stalls down and opened the stall door.

The filly danced in the aisle, arching her neck and flagging her tail. As she tossed her head, Christina could see a snip of white on the end of her dainty nose.

"Come on, Image," the groom said. "I know you'd rather be out playing, but right now I have other things to do besides take you for a walk." With a last playful toss of her head, the filly pranced into her stall. Christina smiled to herself. The arrogant filly was just the kind of horse that would appeal to Melanie. Maybe she'd see if Melanie wanted to visit the stables later.

She turned to walk away when suddenly a bay head shot over the open stall door beside her. Christina had a blurred image of pinned ears, a crooked blaze and bared teeth as a horse lunged at her. She jumped back quickly, the colt's teeth snapping together just where her shoulder had been.

Since many of the racehorses spent nearly twenty-three hours a day in their stalls when they were at the track, they were often territorial and aggressive with strangers. Christina had taken her share of nips, and she had learned to approach new horses slowly, letting them get to know her before she got close to them.

Christina recognized the colt as the one who had dumped Steve, the colt Tommy had referred to as a "suicide ride." She looked around curiously. No one seemed to be paying attention to him. The bay colt rolled his eyes and craned his neck, trying to reach her. She folded her arms across her chest and shook her head. "I didn't mean to get into your space," she said calmly. "Have some manners."

The colt pinned his ears at Christina. When she stood her ground, he flicked his ears uncertainly, then tucked them against his head again.

"You don't scare me, you big fake," she said. In spite of his rolling eyes, he was handsome, with a beautifully shaped head and a strong, graceful neck. She wanted to stroke his crooked blaze, but she didn't dare reach out to the horse. He tucked his nose into his chest and angled his head to eye her closely. After several minutes he relaxed his ears and let his head drop.

"You're much more handsome when you aren't looking so mean," Christina said. "I hear you're really fast, too."

"Yes, he is," a woman's voice said from behind her. "But you're right, he's a horrible, spoiled bully, and it's my fault."

Christina whirled around and found herself facing a well-dressed, middle-aged woman who looked as though she would be right at home watching the races from one of the private suites above the grandstand. Her perfectly styled hair was a soft brown with silvery highlights, and her eyes twinkled in her smooth face. She was wearing a beautiful cream-colored sweater, and light sparkled on the diamonds that dangled from her ears and studded the rings on her fingers.

Christina self-consciously reached up to smooth back her ponytail. She briefly wished she was wearing something nicer than her faded jeans and old T-shirt, but the woman seemed not to take any notice of her clothes.

Her smile was wide and friendly. "Most people don't think much of my Gratis," she said. "It's nice to meet someone who can see through his bad manners."

Christina smiled back. "He's a beautiful horse," she said. "I like him. I'm Christina Reese, by the way."

The colt's owner extended her hand. "I'm Fredericka Graber," the woman said. "I'm pleased to meet you, Christina." Fredericka gazed at the colt and sighed. "Not too many people like Gratis. He can be quite a grump. But he has such speed when he's willing to run, and with his breeding, he should be doing wonderful things. Instead he's spending his time at Turfway terrorizing everyone who walks past his stall."

"What is his breeding?" Christina asked, giving the colt a curious look.

"His sire's grandsire is Affirmed, the Triple Crown

winner," Fredericka said with a broad smile. "My late husband and I bought Gratis's dam at auction. She's an Alydar granddaughter."

"That's the colt Affirmed beat during the Triple Crown races," Christina said. Gratis had amazing bloodlines. She looked at the colt with new interest.

Fredericka nodded. "Quick Promise, the mare, had been ultrasounded and vet-checked before the auction, so imagine our surprise when we brought her home and discovered she was in foal! Since he was free, it seemed fitting to name her colt Gratis."

"Does he have his official works in?" Christina asked, gazing at Gratis, who was watching them intently.

"Oh, yes," Fredericka said. "They were all clocked at Kentucky Downs. Gratis has put in some wonderful times with the young woman who was his regular rider, but she's having a baby and we can't seem to find anyone to replace her." Her voice faded as she looked toward the bay colt. He flicked his ears in her direction. "You're just a surly young man, aren't you?"

Christina could hear Fredericka's affection for her colt, no matter how disagreeable he acted. She immediately liked the colt's owner.

"Do you want to be a jockey someday?" Fredericka asked, looking back at Christina.

"I am a jockey," she replied.

"But you look so young," Fredericka protested.

The black filly down the aisle stuck her head over her door and nickered loudly. Fredericka glanced at her and smiled. "That's my other spoiled two-year-old," she said. "Image. This is her first season at the track and she's quite excited to be here. Would you like to meet her, too?"

"I'd love to, but some other time," Christina said politely, glancing at her watch. "Right now I have to meet my parents at the track—we have some horses running today."

"Well, good luck, and come back and visit anytime," Fredericka said. She headed for the other stall, and Christina started to walk away.

"Are you lost?" Vince Jones's voice made Christina jump. She spun around to face the glowering trainer.

"No," Christina said quickly. "I was just checking on Gratis." She took a breath and braced herself to ask about riding for him.

"Obviously he's fine," Vince said abruptly.

Christina started to turn away, then stopped, looking squarely at the trainer. Her heart thudded in her chest and she took a deep breath. "I wanted to offer to exercise him for you," she said quickly.

Vince rolled his eyes and shook his head, clearly

disgusted. "No bugs," he said flatly. "Now beat it, kid." Then he turned and stomped into his office.

Disappointed, Christina headed for the track. Melanie and Missy were riding in the third race, but Naomi Traeger, Whitebrook's first-call jockey, was riding Raven, one of Whitebrook's two-year-old fillies, in the first race. She found her parents near the paddock, talking with Beth McLean, Ian's pretty, brown-haired wife.

"Where's Ian?" Christina asked, glancing around curiously, trying to spot the tall, redheaded trainer.

"He's at the Keeneland track," Beth said. "Since the two Whitebrook horses running today are Maureen's and your mother's, Ian thought this would be a good time to get some things taken care of before the season opens there next month."

"What about Kevin?" Christina asked.

"He went to Keeneland with his dad," Beth said. "But he'll be here later."

"That's good," Christina said. "Mel and I are supposed to go to dinner with him and Parker tonight."

"We'd better get down to the paddock," Christina's father said, taking her mother by the arm as Maureen led Raven into the viewing paddock.

Naomi and Raven made a bad start, trailing the field by three lengths. But Raven was a come-from-behind horse, and she pulled through in the stretch, winning by a nose. Christina and Ashleigh joined Naomi in the winner's circle, beaming proudly while she was interviewed by the racing press. Then Dani led the sweating black filly away and Naomi headed back to the locker room. She had horses to ride for other barns that day, and she needed to change her silks for her next race.

When Melanie strolled up from the backside with Steve Quinn at her side, Christina tried not to let it annoy her. But when Melanie touched Steve's sleeve and smiled at him, Christina ground her teeth. It was probably a good thing Kevin wasn't there. Christina was sure it would bother him to see Melanie hanging on Steve's every word.

When they reached the paddock, Steve walked to the number seven spot to join his horse's owners. Melanie stopped next to Christina, Ashleigh and Mike at the five position. She gave Christina a tight smile and smoothed the front of her blue-and-white jersey. "Wish me luck," she said.

"You'll be fine," Christina replied.

"I hope so. Steve told me to quit worrying and just have fun," Melanie said.

"Sounds like good advice," Christina said, trying to keep her voice neutral.

Maureen stopped Missy in front of them, and Mike gave Melanie a leg up. As Maureen handed the filly off to the pony rider, Christina found herself crossing the fingers on both hands. *You can do this, Mel,* she said to herself. *I know you can.*

She held her breath as the last of the horses was loaded into the starting gate. She leaned on the rail, her eyes locked on the number five chute, and when the starting bell sounded, Christina thought her heart was going to jump into her throat. This was it!

But as the horses charged out of the gate, Christina could see Melanie holding Missy back. Christina clenched her fists in frustration as Melanie let one chance after another to move into a better position slip past her. Christina was sure it was only because of Missy's experience and speed that they managed to cross the finish line in third place.

When Melanie came off the track she handed Missy to Maureen, then, without a word to anyone, headed for the locker room.

Christina started after her, but Ashleigh stopped her. "Let her go, Chris," she said. "She looks like she could use some time to herself."

Christina knew her mother was right, but it was hard to do nothing when she could see how upset her cousin was. She forced herself to watch the next few races, but her mind was elsewhere. What if Melanie never lost her bug? What if *she* never lost her bug?

Then, near the rail, she spotted Fredericka Graber and Vince Jones deep in conversation. Fredericka glanced up and waved when she saw her, and Christina waved back.

"Somehow," she murmured to herself, "I'm going to ride Gratis. And I'll show Vince Jones that just because I'm a bug doesn't mean I can't ride."

4

"ASHLEIGH GRIFFEN, HOW GOOD TO SEE YOU AGAIN."

Christina's jaw went slack as Fredericka Graber walked up to her mother. To Christina's growing amazement, the two women hugged each other. Then Fredericka turned to Mike. "You're looking well, Michael. I understand the two of you are doing nicely with your breeding operation."

"We're working at it," Mike said modestly.

"You all know each other?" Christina asked.

"Your mother jockeyed a few racehorses for my husband and me," Fredericka said. "You didn't tell me your mother was Ashleigh Griffen, Christina."

"It's been years since we've seen you, Fredericka," Ashleigh said. "I heard you'd gone to Florida for a while. How are you doing?"

Fredericka's bright smile faded a little. "It was difficult when Charles first passed away," she said. "But having the horses has kept me very busy. Vince is doing a wonderful job training my racers. He's such a sweet man."

Christina stifled a laugh. *Sweet? Vince Jones?* She wondered if Fredericka was talking about the same Vince Jones who spent most of his time yelling at people.

"Do you still own Townsend Mistress?" Ashleigh asked.

Christina's attention darted from her mother to Fredericka.

Fredericka nodded. "Brad Townsend is just beside himself over selling her so quickly," she said.

"Mistress is a granddaughter of Townsend Holly," Ashleigh explained to Christina.

"Holly was Wonder's dam," Christina told Fredericka.

"I know," the older woman said. "I watched your mother race Wonder in the Derby. After we saw that race, my husband was determined to have a horse just like Wonder. Mistress was as close as he got."

"How is she doing?" Ashleigh asked.

"So well that Brad keeps trying to buy her back," Fredericka said. She glanced at Christina. "Mistress

52

had trouble delivering her first foal, and Brad made the decision to get rid of her rather than try breeding her again. We've had three lovely foals out of her. You saw her last filly, the black one that Vince has here."

"Image?" No wonder the filly looked so great. She had some of the same bloodlines Star had.

Then another thought crossed Christina's mind. "Has Vince found another rider for Gratis yet?" she asked.

Fredericka gave her a sharp look. "Not that I know of," she said. "Vince wants to get him to run with a man on him, but I'm sure it will need to be a woman, someone with the right temperament and plenty of patience to work with my big, spoiled grump. But Vince is the expert. I'm sure he'll figure it out."

"He'd be an awesome horse to ride," Christina commented.

Fredericka glanced at her watch. "I need to run. I have a business meeting to attend. It was delightful to see you again, Ashleigh." She turned to Christina. "I'm going to speak to Vince," she said. "Maybe he'll give you a chance on Gratis. Of course," she added, "all the training decisions are up to him."

"Thank you," Christina said.

Fredericka walked away, and Ashleigh glanced at Christina. "Didn't you say you and Melanie had a date this afternoon with the boys? You'd better go change."

"We're going to eat at that diner near the motel," Christina said. "Don't worry, Parker and Kevin will drop us off after we eat."

"That's fine," Ashleigh said. "We'll be in our room if you need us." Mike and Ashleigh were staying in the room adjoining Christina and Melanie's. On Sunday night Mike would return to Whitebrook, leaving Ashleigh and the girls in Florence for the week.

Christina headed for the lockers. She didn't have much time before Parker and Kevin would arrive. She was looking forward to seeing her boyfriend for the first time all week, and she wanted to look nice for him.

She found Melanie in the TV room with a few other jockeys, including Steve Quinn. Christina bit her lower lip and looked directly at Melanie, doing her best to ignore Steve.

"Parker and Kevin are going to be here in a few minutes. Shouldn't we get ready to go?"

She turned without another word and headed for the locker room. Melanie came in right behind her. The girls showered and dressed without saying anything. Melanie pulled on a bright yellow T-shirt and black flared pants, then slipped into a pair of platform shoes that added a few inches to her short frame.

Christina tucked her pink tank top into the waistband of her jean skirt and slipped on a pair of sandals. The girls stood side by side, applying lip gloss and fixing their hair. "You look nice," Christina said finally, to break the silence.

"Thanks," Melanie said. "You too. I like that skirt on you."

They hurried out of the locker room and through the jockey room. Outside, Kevin McLean was leaning against the side of the building, gazing up at the cloudless sky, his T-shirt tucked neatly into his black jeans, his red hair slightly wind-tousled. Parker Townsend stood nearby, wearing tan slacks and a button-down shirt, his suede jacket flung over one shoulder, his dark hair freshly combed.

Christina hurried to Parker's side, rising up on her toes to kiss him lightly on the cheek. Parker wrapped his arm around her shoulder. "You look great," he said.

"You too," Christina replied, smiling up at him.

"Let's go," Melanie said, lifting her chin so that Kevin could give her a kiss.

Parker took Christina's duffel bag, but as they started across the backside toward the parking lot, Christina noticed that Melanie carried her own bag, holding it between her and Kevin.

There were only a few patrons in the diner, so the

hostess seated the foursome at a large, quiet table near the back of the room. Music from the local country-western radio station twanged and whined from a stereo behind the counter.

Kevin rolled his eyes and groaned. "Whoever wrote 'It's Been Lonesome in the Saddle Since My Horse Died' wasn't the greatest lyricist in the world, that's for sure."

Parker and Christina laughed, but Melanie just stared intently at the menu.

After they placed their orders, Parker leaned back in his chair, draping his arm across Christina's shoulders.

"How are things going at Sam's?" Christina asked, turning to him. "How's Foxy? And how are Kaitlin and Sterling doing?" When she had made the decision to pursue racing, Christina had sold her eventing mare, Sterling Dream, to Kevin's older sister, Samantha Nelson. Sam and her husband, Tor, ran Whisperwood, a training facility for event riders. A classmate of Christina and Melanie's, Kaitlin Boyce, was leasing Sterling, and she was just starting to compete.

"Oh, I'm fine. Thanks for asking," Parker teased her.

Christina punched him lightly in the arm. "I can see that," she said affectionately. "Is Kaitlin doing okay with Sterling?"

"Sterling is going great," he said. "You'd be proud of her."

"As soon as we get back to Lexington, I have to go see her," Christina said.

"We're doing a clinic next month," Parker said. An experienced three-day-event rider, he worked for Sam and Tor, helping train novice riders, while he pursued his own riding career. "You could come see Kaitlin ride Sterling then."

"Okay," Christina said. "Will you ride Foxy at the clinic?" Parker often used his bay mare to demonstrate techniques while Samantha instructed her students.

"Probably not," Parker said. "But we're going to compete next weekend at Stonecrest Farm. Any chance you can come watch?"

Christina's shoulders sagged. "I have races both Saturday and Sunday," she said. "Mom is going to be busy, and without a ride, there's no way I can get over there."

"You two have to get your licenses," Kevin said, tilting his chair back.

"That isn't going to happen until we have time to take driver's ed," Melanie said.

Christina eyed Kevin and Melanie from across the table. Neither of them seemed to have much to say, and Melanie kept her gaze focused on the tabletop.

"School's starting up in a couple of weeks, and we're both planning to take driver's ed right away," Christina said quickly, frowning at Melanie's downcast expression. "It's going to be fun, right, Mel?"

"School," Melanie groaned. "I keep trying to forget about it."

"Why?" Parker asked. "Aren't you excited to be a senior?"

"I used to think I couldn't wait," Melanie said, arranging her silverware into a triangle. "But now I don't want this to be my last year of high school. I mean, do you miss high school at all?" she asked Parker.

"No way," Parker said. "It's great to be able to ride all the time, anytime."

"Have you thought about what you're going to do next year, Kevin?" Christina asked, trying to pull him into the conversation.

Kevin shrugged, pulling sugar packets from the holder on the table and propping them into little tents. "I'd like to play soccer at a good college," he said. "I still haven't figured out what I would study, though. Maybe teaching, so that when I graduate I can have summers off."

When Melanie didn't even look up at Kevin, Christina frowned, eyeing her two friends. They'd hardly spoken to each other since leaving Turfway.

"Did you get your class schedule yet?" she asked Kevin. The evening wasn't going to be much fun if Kevin and Melanie weren't talking to each other.

"It came in the mail yesterday," he said. "I have sociology, advanced calculus, PE, and speech. Should be an easy trimester."

The waitress set a basket of crackers and breadsticks on the table. Melanie broke a breadstick in two, then set it aside without tasting it. "I don't think we'll have any classes together," she said. "I'm not in advanced anything."

"Oh, well," Kevin said, sounding nonchalant. "It isn't like you ever have much time for me anyway."

Melanie's expression darkened.

To Christina's relief, the waitress brought their food before Melanie could respond to Kevin's comment.

"Parker," she said as the waitress walked away, "what do you know about Fredericka Graber?"

Parker frowned thoughtfully. "I've heard my dad mention the name. Why?"

As they began eating, Christina told them about Fredericka, Townsend Mistress, Image and Gratis. "Mrs. Graber said she'd have a talk with Vince Jones," she said excitedly. "I may get a chance to exercise-ride for him." Her excitement faded a little when she saw

Melanie's face. Her cousin looked so dejected, quietly picking at the croutons on her Caesar salad.

"You have to see this filly, Mel," she said quickly. "Want to go over to Vince's stables with me in the morning?"

Melanie shrugged. "Sure," she said neutrally. "But the way things are going for me right now, I'll never get a chance to ride a horse for a trainer like Vince."

"You're going to have a good ride tomorrow," Christina said, smiling at her cousin. "You and Missy were just a little off today. Tomorrow will be better." At least she hoped so, for Melanie's sake. "Mel's racing Rascal," Christina announced to Parker and Kevin. "It's going to be a great race, isn't it, Mel?" she asked with forced cheerfulness.

But Melanie said nothing, her attention riveted on spearing a piece of olive with her fork.

Christina heaved a sigh of relief when they left the restaurant. Trying to keep a conversation going when Melanie and Kevin had been as sociable as a couple of stumps had been so draining.

When the boys dropped them off at the motel, Parker leaned across the seat and took her hand. "I miss you, you know," he said quietly. "I don't like not seeing you every day."

Christina gazed into his face and smiled warmly. "I

know," she said. "I miss you, too. But I'll be home in a couple of weeks, and we'll have more time then."

Parker gave her a light kiss and then released her hand. "I'll talk to you soon, okay?"

Christina and Melanie climbed out of the car, and Christina waved goodbye as Parker and Kevin drove away. Then she followed Melanie into their drab little room and dropped her purse on her bed. Melanie went straight to the bathroom, coming out a few minutes later in her oversized nightshirt. Without a word to Christina, she climbed into her bed and turned the lamp off.

Christina gazed at her cousin's still form for a moment, then sighed. She couldn't force Melanie to talk to her. She got ready for bed, worrying over Melanie's race the next day. Her cousin had been acting strange for the last few weeks, but she had seemed really out of sorts that evening. Christina hoped Melanie would have her mind on her race the next afternoon. She didn't need another unremarkable finish, like the one she'd had that day.

Christina climbed into bed and pulled the covers up over her shoulders. As she began to drift off, she envisioned herself on Star, crossing the finish line in first place in the Breeder's Futurity. A smile tugged at the corners of her mouth. She and Star would win. She knew they could. Then her sleepy mind wandered to Gratis, replaying the scene on the track that morning. She fell asleep and dreamed that a red-faced Vince Jones was screaming at her angrily as the bay colt bucked his way down the track, with Christina clinging helplessly to the saddle.

It was still dark Sunday morning when Ashleigh met Christina and Melanie in front of the motel. "You guys got in early last night," she said. "It couldn't have been later than seven when Parker and Kevin dropped you off."

"Nice to know that you're spying on us, Mom. Parker needed to get back to Lexington," Christina said. "And since Mel is racing today, we didn't want to stay out very late. It's hard to get up at four in the morning no matter how early you go to bed!"

"I know," Ashleigh said. "So, are you both ready for a busy day?"

"I have five horses to work this morning," Christina said, buckling her seat belt.

"Star first, though, right?" Ashleigh asked.

"Of course, Mom," Christina replied. "Star always comes first."

"What about you, Melanie?" Ashleigh glanced over her shoulder to look at Melanie, who had settled onto the backseat and was gazing out the window.

"I have four horses to exercise this morning," Melanie said. "Two for Lawrence Smith's stables and two for Mark Meyer. Then nothing until the afternoon."

"You'll have time to go see Mrs. Graber's filly with me, then," Christina said, twisting in her seat to look at her cousin.

Melanie shrugged, still gazing out the window. "Sure."

Ashleigh turned onto the road to the racetrack. "I'd like to see her, too," she said, not seeming to notice Melanie's neutral response. "You know, Mel," Ashleigh continued, "this afternoon, when you and Rascal come out of the gate . . ."

Christina was startled to see Melanie flinch when Ashleigh mentioned the race. As her mother continued to coach Melanie, Christina watched her cousin's face grow pale. Melanie stayed rigid and quiet while Ashleigh instructed her on how best to ride the colt.

When Ashleigh pulled into the parking area

behind the barns, Melanie quickly climbed out of the car and hurried toward the jockey room. Christina followed slowly, frowning at her cousin's back. Was Melanie going to be able to handle that day's race, Christina wondered, or should she say something to her mother before it was too late?

The women's locker room was busy, and Christina couldn't talk to Melanie privately before her cousin left for the track. By the time Christina had Star ready to go, dawn was barely breaking. Grooms and trainers checked stalls and led horses out to be saddled for their works as Christina led Star toward the oval.

"Just jog him an easy couple of miles today," Ashleigh said when she met her at the rail. "I know the vet said his legs looked good, but I want to take it easy for a few days and not stress him at all."

Melanie was on the track on a gray colt, but she was moving at a fast trot. Christina held Star to a slow jog. The colt's ears were pricked and each step was loaded with energy. Christina was dying to let him run, but she resisted, knowing her mother's training methods were both safe and wise. By the time they were done with their workout, the sky was getting light and the air was warming up.

June Fortig was waiting by the track when Christina reached the rail. "I'll have Dani put Star up," her mother said. "I'll see you at the stalls later."

"Thanks, Mom," Christina said, turning to the solid black filly one of June's handlers was holding, waiting for her to mount up.

"This is Dark Wind," June said, patting the filly's sleek neck. "I want you to jog her a mile, then move her up to a nice, easy canter for another mile, then we'll cool her out. Windy hasn't been on the track here yet, so you might need to coddle her a little."

"Sure thing," Christina said, letting June give her a leg up. She settled onto the filly's back and collected the reins. June escorted her to the gap, then stepped back as Christina turned the filly along the rail.

The workout went perfectly, with the filly eagerly listening to everything Christina asked her to do. When they were done, she hopped to the ground, a broad grin splitting her face. "She was an angel," she exclaimed to June.

June nodded, looking pleased. "I'll have another horse up in a few minutes, if you want to stick around."

Christina leaned against the rail, watching a jockey canter by on a handsome chestnut.

"Christina!"

She looked over her shoulder to see Fredericka striding toward her. Gratis's owner stopped beside her and offered an apologetic smile. "I'm here to watch Gratis work," she said. "Vince has a rider he thinks can handle him."

"That's good," Christina said, barely hiding the disappointment in her voice.

"I know you'd be perfect for him," Fredericka continued, "but Vince is the trainer, after all."

"I understand," Christina said, turning back to the rail as a commotion broke out near the gap.

"Oh, dear," Fredericka said softly. "I think that's my horse."

Through the half-light of the early morning, she could see a horse fighting its handler. She watched the colt rear, striking at his handler. The man moved away from the flailing hooves, trying to bring Gratis back down to the ground.

Beside Christina, Fredericka sighed. "Vince said he wants Gratis to get used to being handled by men. He can't always have a woman available. But I think Gratis disagrees."

Christina understood what Vince was trying to do—getting Gratis to work no matter who was on him. A horse that would work for only one jockey was pretty limited. Ashleigh worried about the same thing with Star, that Christina might not always be there to race him. But until they could find another rider that

Star would perform equally well with, he'd be a one-jockey horse. Christina didn't mind. She loved being the person Star trusted most, and she wanted to ride him forever and ever.

"Give me that lead," Vince snapped, snatching Gratis's line from the groom.

"I don't know what got into him, Mr. Jones," the groom said. "He seemed like he was going to be okay, and then he just went off."

Christina watched as Vince brought the colt under control with a firm and expert hand. But the exercise rider shook his head. "No way," he said to Vince. "No money in the world is going to get me on that horse."

Christina could feel Fredericka gazing at her, but before she could say anything, June Fortig's handler was walking toward her again, a bay colt in hand.

"I have a horse to work," Christina said quickly. After seeing Gratis acting so wild again, she wasn't sure she wanted to ride him after all. Was he safe?

The bay colt went nicely for her, though he felt a little sluggish. When she came off the track with him, Pam Mahony had a horse ready to go, and then another. After working Pam's horses, Christina headed back to the locker room. As she walked by Vince Jones, the trainer stepped away from the rail, where he was watching another of his horses work.

She paused, waiting for him to speak.

"Not bad riding," he said, then turned away.

Christina frowned at his back for a minute. *"Not bad"? That's it?* When he kept his back to her, she walked away, perplexed by the man's behavior. She hurried to the locker room, looking for Melanie, but her cousin was nowhere in sight. Christina showered, then checked the jockey room once again, asking some of the other jockeys if they had seen her cousin. But no one had. Maybe she had forgotten about going over to Vince Jones's stables, Christina thought. She left, stopping by the track kitchen to buy an apple before heading for Whitebrook's stables. Star was already in his stall, his coat gleaming from the bath Dani had given him after his work.

"Hello, handsome," Christina crooned, slipping into his stall. She sank her teeth into the apple, tearing a large chunk off it, and handed the bite to Star.

When he was done with the apple, Christina wrapped her arms around the colt's neck, pressing her face into his mane. Star heaved a contented sigh. "We're going to win the Futurity, aren't we, boy?" she murmured, running her hand along his powerful shoulder. "And next year it'll be you and me in the Triple Crown, right?"

Star blew out noisily, then snuffled up and down

her back, hunting for another apple.

"You don't care what race we're running in, do you, silly?" she asked, stepping back. "You just like to run and win."

Christina had two races scheduled for the afternoon. When she came out of the gate in her first race, a claiming race for maiden fillies and mares, the bay filly she was on was hesitant. Christina had to push the animal to keep up with the field, and finished a disappointing fourth. To her relief, the trainer was still pleased with the filly's performance, and offered Christina rides on other horses.

In Christina's second race, she got the gray mare she was riding out of the gate ahead of the field. Although the field was full of good runners, she managed to keep the mare running in front right up until the last furlong, ending in second place. After the race Christina hurried back to the locker room to get out of her silks. She saw Melanie talking with Steve Quinn in the jockey room, and walked past her without saying anything. When she came out of the shower, the locker room was full of jockeys. Melanie was pulling on a blue-and-white Whitebrook jersey, but she had her back to Christina, who left the crowded room without trying to speak to Mel. If she wanted to hang around with people like Steve, that was her business.

When Christina reached the viewing paddock her parents were already in the ring, waiting for Melanie. As the horses were led into the saddling area, Christina eyed the competition closely. A blood bay called Comanche Trail looked like the most likely contender for first place. The odds boards seemed to agree, as his numbers stayed low at three to one. The horse tossed his head, flipping his black mane in the air as he pranced around the viewing paddock. "He looks really good," Christina said, biting her lower lip.

"Yes, he does," Mike said. "His times indicate he's a great sprinter, but I doubt he can hold his speed for a mile."

"I'm hoping Rascal can outrun him the whole way. Melanie will be so upset if she doesn't get a win soon. This is really getting to her."

Melanie strode into the paddock, buckling the chin strap of her helmet as she stopped next to Christina.

"Steve thinks you're using Mrs. Graber to talk Vince into letting you ride Gratis," she said to Christina, adjusting her helmet to a close fit.

"What? I never even asked her to talk to him!" Christina exclaimed, staring at Melanie in disbelief.

"I didn't say you did," Melanie replied. "I'm just telling you what Steve said."

Christina pressed her lips together. She couldn't believe Melanie was repeating the stupid things Steve Quinn told her, but she wasn't going to get in a fight with her cousin just before the race. It had to be Melanie's nerves that were making her act this way. She wasn't being herself at all.

When Dani led Rascal in, Mike gave Melanie a leg up onto the chestnut colt's back.

"This is it," Melanie said, glancing down at Christina. "We're going to win this one."

"Good luck," Christina said as Dani walked Rascal across to join the pony rider.

Christina followed her mother over to the track. Fans thronged around them, and Christina squeezed into a space at the rail, her stomach knotted with tension. Ashleigh stood beside her, gripping the rail with both hands. They watched in silence as the horses paraded toward the starting gate.

When they broke from the gate, Christina was relieved to see Melanie doing as Ashleigh and Maureen had instructed her—holding Rascal back until they got closer to the finish.

Comanche Trail took an early lead, but Christina remembered what her father had said about the horse being a good sprinter. "His fractions are amazing," she said, watching the big bay tear down the far side of the track. "There's no way he can keep it up." To her relief, the colt slowed as he came onto the straight stretch on the far side, and the rest of the field caught up with him.

The roar of the crowd grew as the horses came into the second turn. Christina rose to her toes as Melanie shifted her position. "She's making her move now," she said, watching her cousin maneuver around a pair of chestnuts and a gray, then inch up on Comanche Trail. Melanie seemed to be riding confidently. Ashleigh had been right to put her on Rascal.

When she asked for more from the colt, Rascal moved up beside Comanche Trail, and then they were coming out of the turn. Melanie cued Rascal to switch leads as they came onto the straight stretch, and Christina whooped as they passed Comanche Trail and took the lead. "She's going to do it," she cried, grabbing her mother's arm and pounding her fist on the rail. "They're going to win!"

But at the last pole she watched Comanche Trail flip up his ears as his jockey shifted his weight on the colt's back. The big Thoroughbred dug in and pulled up beside Rascal, then crossed the finish line a half stride ahead.

"No!" Ashleigh exhaled sharply as the numbers flashed onto the board. "Poor Melanie."

Christina stared at the finish order. Melanie was second. Again.

She hurried toward the backside to be there when Melanie left the track. She wasn't looking forward to seeing the look on Melanie's face.

Fredericka was standing by the rail. "What a shame that your horse came in second," she said, looking at Ashleigh. "He certainly ran a good race."

"Yes," Ashleigh said. "It was definitely disappointing, but they made a good show."

Christina knew her mother was talking about Melanie and not Rascal. She kept her eyes on the track as Melanie and Rascal circled back. Her cousin looked distraught, and Christina could see that Melanie needed her. She took a step toward the track to meet them.

"Before you go, I would like to talk to you about Gratis," Fredericka said.

Ashleigh flicked a glance at Christina. "I'd better go talk to Mel," she said.

"I'll be there right away," Christina said as her mother hurried away.

"I just spoke with Vince," Fredericka said. "He'd like to talk to you. Are you free to visit the backside right now?"

Melanie and Ashleigh walked by together. From

Melanie's face, which was rigid and unsmiling, Christina guessed that her cousin didn't want too many people hanging over her at the moment.

"Sure. Now is fine," Christina said. She followed as Fredericka led the way to Vince's stables, and stopped at the trainer's office door. Christina paused outside the doorway, too.

Vince glanced up from his desk, which was cluttered with papers, copies of the *Daily Racing Form*, condition books, and schedules. He had a dour expression on his sun-lined face.

"Mrs. Graber and I would like you to exercise Gratis," he said, not looking very happy about offering her the job. "He's supposed to race next weekend in one of the Breeders' Cup races. I'd like to get him working before then."

Christina felt her jaw go slack. Vince Jones was offering her the chance to ride for him. Only in her wildest dreams had she ever thought this would happen.

She glanced at Fredericka, who stood by the door with an expectant look on her face. Christina caught her lower lip in her teeth, thinking about Gratis and how potentially dangerous he was. But riding for Vince Jones was the opportunity of a lifetime. How could she turn him down?

"I'd love to," she said finally, her mind racing. If she could handle the colt, maybe Vince would consider naming her as his jockey for the race!

"We'll put you on him after the races this afternoon," Vince said brusquely. "Can you manage that?"

When Christina nodded, Vince rubbed his chin with his thumb. "I'll have a pony rider escort you on the track," he said. "We'll just have to play it by ear until we know how he's going to behave for you."

Christina nodded mutely, wondering what she had just gotten herself into. Melanie was the one with the knack for problem horses, not she. But she wasn't going to back out now. This was her chance to show Vince Jones she was a competent jockey, even if she was just a bug.

"I'll meet you here at four," Vince said. Christina nodded again, mumbling her thanks, and headed out the door, catching Mrs. Graber's gleeful wink as she passed by.

She stopped short when she rounded the corner, where Gratis was standing at the wash rack. A young woman was reaching past the colt to grab a rag. Gratis rolled his eyes back and bared his teeth, snapping at the girl. She ducked quickly, avoiding the bite, but Christina felt a heaviness settle on her. Maybe it wasn't just men Gratis didn't like.

She remembered what the vet had said, that Gratis didn't have the mind to be a racehorse. Maybe just being around the track excitement was what set him off. And if that was the case, she didn't have a ghost of a chance to prove herself to Vince. Gratis would make sure of it.

6

CHRISTINA WALKED AWAY FROM GRATIS, HER MIND whirling with images from her disturbing dream the night before and from the sight of the colt, his wicked teeth bared as he lunged at the groom. She had to have been out of her mind to agree to get on him.

"There you are!" Ashleigh strode along the shedrow toward her, a worried look on her face.

"What's wrong?" Christina asked, hurrying to her mother.

"It's Melanie," Ashleigh said, steering Christina toward the building that housed the jockey room. "Maybe you can talk to her, Chris. She's so distraught, and there doesn't seem to be anything I can say that helps."

"But what can I say?" Christina asked. "You're the experienced jockey. If she won't listen to you, what could I possibly tell her?"

Ashleigh cocked her head, looking at Christina. "Just let her know she still has a best friend, Chris. Right now I think Mel's feeling pretty much alone."

Ashleigh left Christina at the door to the jockey room, and Christina hurried to the locker room, where she found her cousin sitting on a bench, staring at the wall of lockers in front of her. Vicky Frontiere and another jockey, Jean Bennett, were just leaving the room. They both shook their heads when they saw her.

Vicky had a worried frown creasing her brow. "Good luck," she mouthed to Christina as she followed Jean out the door.

Christina gnawed at her lower lip while she eyed Melanie's back. Finally she took a deep breath and crossed the room to sit on the bench beside Melanie.

"What can I do, Mel?" she asked in a quiet voice.

"Nothing," Melanie said. "There's nothing you can do. My life is terrible."

"What is it that Kevin always says?" Christina asked. "His little quote about how if we always had sunshine in our lives, the world would look like the Sahara Desert?"

At the mention of Kevin's name, Melanie burst into tears.

"Oh, Mel, what's going on?" Christina demanded. "Please tell me. What's wrong?"

"Kevin," Melanie said. "He doesn't care about me anymore."

"What are you talking about?" Christina asked, puzzled. She thought back to their dinner the night before. "But he was here with Parker last night."

"And he didn't say two whole sentences to me," Melanie said.

Christina exhaled. From what she had seen, Melanie hadn't had much to say to Kevin, either. "I know he cares about you, Mel," she said in a reassuring voice. "I'm sure it's been hard on him to have you gone so much this summer. Things will get better."

"I don't know," Melanie murmured, sitting up and swiping at her eyes with the back of her hand. "I think he's tired of hearing about all the times I lose, too. It isn't exactly exciting, you know."

"You rode a great race today," Christina said. "You and Rascal looked really good out there."

"I stank," Melanie replied in a low voice. "I lost. Again."

"You didn't stink!" Christina protested.

"If someone else had been riding him, Rascal could

have won," Melanie replied, her shoulders slumping a little more.

Christina rolled her head back and groaned. "And if Comanche Trail's jockey had been half a pound heavier, you could have won, and if the track had been a little softer or a little harder . . ." She shook her head. "Stop beating yourself up, Melanie! You're a great jockey."

"I'm a bug," Melanie snapped. "And I'll be a bug for my whole, short racing career."

"What are you talking about?" Christina stared at her cousin.

"I'll never win another race as long as I ride," Melanie said, her voice catching. "And I'll never lose my bug. Ever since that wreck at Ellis Park, it's been harder and harder to race."

"I don't get it," Christina said, frowning. "You got right back in the saddle the next day. It wasn't like you suddenly lost your nerve."

Melanie closed her eyes and sighed heavily. "That's what I thought, too," she said. "That if I could get back on, I'd be fine. But it isn't working, Chris." She choked back a sob and sniffed. "Every time I get on a horse I start thinking it could be my next wreck. I keep feeling myself hitting the ground, feeling that horse's hoof hit the back of my helmet, and I get more and more tense.

It's getting worse instead of better."

Christina thought back to Missy's race, when Melanie had avoided making any bold moves. She had thrown away any chances that might have meant a solid win for the filly. But her ride on Rascal had been much different—they really had almost won.

"It didn't show today," Christina countered. "You and Rascal both looked pretty competitive."

Melanie shrugged. "Rascal wasn't making it easy for me," she said. "I was so busy working at keeping him under control that I didn't have time to worry. I guess I forgot to be so afraid, but I lost anyway."

Christina gazed thoughtfully at her cousin. "Rascal made you ride better by making things tough for you?"

Melanie wrinkled her nose. "I guess," she said. She rubbed at her damp cheek. "It isn't like I can't handle the horse," she said. "It's thinking about everything that could happen around us." She rose. "I need to go wash up," she said. "There'll be more jockeys coming in any minute, and I don't want them to see me like this."

The locker room door swung open, and Ashleigh stuck her head inside the room. "Chris," she said, "I need to see you for a minute."

"You're okay, right?" Christina looked at Melanie.

Melanie gave her a thin smile and nodded. "Thanks, Chris. I'll be fine." Melanie headed for the row of sinks, and Christina followed her mother through the jockey room and outside.

Ashleigh stopped outside the door, turning to face Christina, a serious expression on her face. "I think I've come up with a way to help Melanie," she said. "But it depends a lot on you."

"Me?" Christina asked. "Sure. If you really think it will help Melanie, I'm all for it, whatever it is."

"I'm glad you feel that way," Ashleigh said. "Because what I want to do is have Melanie start working with Star again."

7

CHRISTINA STARED AT HER MOTHER. "MELANIE AND STAR? You're kidding, right?" She leaned against the side of the building, shaking her head. "Melanie needs a horse she can really work with, Mom. You already tried to put her and Star together, remember? She had an awful time with him!"

Earlier in the summer Melanie had tried to ride Star, but it hadn't worked out at all. They were both too headstrong, and after only a few attempts to ride the colt, both Melanie and Ashleigh had given up the idea.

"Don't you think you should try her with a horse you know she has a chance with? I think putting her on Star might discourage her even more."

With the Breeder's Futurity less than two weeks away, Christina thought changing Star's routine wasn't going to do him any good. But Christina knew she was being selfish, too; she couldn't say it, but she really didn't want her cousin to ride Star.

Ashleigh gazed steadily at Christina, a determined look on her face. "What did you notice about today's race, compared to the one Melanie rode yesterday?"

Christina looked down at her hands. "That Mel did better with Rascal than she did with Missy," she finally said. "But that could have been the coaching you gave her," she added quickly. "She was just following your instructions."

"It wasn't just that, Chris," Ashleigh said. "Maureen and I talked about it, and she saw the same thing I did."

Melanie had said it in the locker room, too. Christina didn't want to admit it, but she knew Ashleigh had identified Melanie's problem. And she knew her mother had come up with the best possible solution.

"I saw it, too, Mom," she said slowly, looking up to meet her mother's eyes. "Mel said it was because Rascal is such a handful, and she was too busy managing him to worry about anything else. She almost won that race. She really did."

"That's what I think, too," Ashleigh said. "That's why I want her to start exercising Star."

In spite of how possessive she was about Star, Christina nodded in agreement. If there was a chance that riding Star would help Melanie regain her confidence, they had to try it. "Do you still want me to ride him in the Futurity?" she asked tentatively.

"Of course," Ashleigh said. "But you're okay with Mel exercising him?"

Christina nodded slowly. "Sure," she said. "I hate seeing her so down on herself. But," she added, "it's really up to Mel. I don't know if she'll go for it."

"Let me take care of that," Ashleigh said. "Let's go talk to her right now." As they turned to head back inside, Melanie appeared at the door. In spite of her freshly washed face, her eyes were still red-rimmed and puffy-looking.

"Just the person we wanted to see," Ashleigh said cheerfully.

"About what?" Melanie asked, looking from Ashleigh to Christina.

"A little schedule change," Ashleigh said. "Tomorrow morning I want you to start working Star."

Melanie's jaw dropped, and she stared at Ashleigh, shaking her head slowly. "I don't think so, Aunt Ashleigh. That's a really bad idea."

Christina was almost relieved to hear Melanie disagree with her mother. She'd still prefer to work Star herself. Maybe they could find another horse for Melanie to work.

But Ashleigh pressed her lips together and dropped her chin, looking from Christina to Melanie.

Christina knew her mother's stubborn expression well. Melanie was going to end up on Star, no matter how much she argued about it. Ashleigh was the trainer, after all, and she would get her way.

"I realize Star can be demanding," Ashleigh said. She grinned at Melanie. "I rode him last month, too, you know. It's going to be a challenge for you to win his trust," Ashleigh continued. "But I think exercising Star will force you to concentrate on getting the horse to go well rather than worrying about hitting the ground. You're a natural rider, Mel. You need to get back to that and stop thinking so much. Rascal helped prove that today."

Melanie's gaze shifted from Ashleigh's face to Christina's. Christina smiled at her cousin and nodded. "It's not even about horses anymore, Mel. It's a parent thing," she said with a laugh. "You know how they say it's for your own good?"

"You guys are serious?" Melanie said. "You really want me to work with Star?"

"Yes," Ashleigh said. "Star may be just what you need to turn things around on the track."

"It's worth a try, isn't it, Mel?" Christina asked. She anticipated another protest from Melanie, but her cousin didn't look as though she wanted to argue. In fact, she looked a little hopeful.

"You're the boss," Melanie said to Ashleigh.

"It's settled, then," Ashleigh said, glancing at her watch. "Now, the last race of the day is going to start in just a minute. Do you two want to go watch it?"

Christina clapped her hand over her mouth. "No! I completely forgot to tell you! I'm taking a colt out for Vince Jones after the track is cleared."

Ashleigh narrowed her eyes. "What colt?" she asked.

"Mrs. Graber's bay colt," Christina said quickly, then waited for her mother's reaction.

Ashleigh frowned deeply. "The bay colt that was flipped on the track yesterday? Do you think that's such a good idea, Chris? He looks pretty unreliable."

"He doesn't always act like that, Mom." Christina hoped she wasn't lying, but after having seen Gratis act up again earlier, she wondered if it was possible he could behave even worse. "This is my chance to really prove myself. Please don't say no."

Ashleigh hesitated long enough that Christina was

sure her mother was going to say she couldn't ride Gratis. But after several seconds Ashleigh sighed.

"Just be careful, okay?"

"Of course I will, Mom," Christina promised. "I'd better get over to Vince's stable. I want to help tack Gratis up."

She hurried away, so excited over riding Gratis she'd almost completely forgotten that Melanie was going to be working with Star.

When she arrived at Vince's stabling area, Gratis was in the aisle. There was a groom on either side of him with a tight grip on his headstall, while a third groom was fastening the girth. Gratis had his ears pressed tightly against his head, his body stiff—ready to break free.

Christina stood back, watching the handlers struggle with the agitated horse. Worried thoughts paraded through her head. *Maybe riding Gratis isn't such a great idea. I could just walk away.* But deep down she knew she couldn't.

"Sure you're up to this?"

She glanced over her shoulder to see Vince Jones standing behind her. His gaze flicked from the fractious colt to her, and Christina stiffened her spine at his doubtful expression.

"Of course I am," she said. "Just give me a minute."

The groom finished with the girth, and Christina walked to Gratis's head. She stood to the side, out of striking range of his hooves.

"Hey, grouchy," she said in a light voice. The colt rolled his eyes in her direction, his ears still pinned, his nostrils flared. With his head flung high in the air, he looked massive—and dangerous.

Christina exhaled and took a step closer to Gratis's shoulder. "Can you let loose of his head a little?" she asked the groom. "I think that might be making him more tense."

The groom looked at Vince. From the corner of her eye, Christina saw the trainer nod slightly. She grimaced. He was probably just waiting to see how big a bite Gratis would take of her.

When the groom eased his hold on the colt, Gratis swung his nose down toward Christina, his teeth bared. But when he caught her scent, he jerked to a stop.

"There," she said, sighing with relief. "See, you really don't want to hurt me."

Gratis snorted loudly, then dropped his head a little, shoving his nose in her direction. His ears stayed up, so Christina cautiously held out her hand, letting the colt snuffle it. She held her breath as he shoved his nose against her palm.

He snorted even more loudly, then jerked his head up and struck at the ground. Christina didn't move, and in a few seconds Gratis dropped his head again to snuffle at her hand.

Slowly Christina reached up with her other hand and gently rubbed the colt's nose. Gratis wiggled his upper lip on her palm, and Christina felt elated. The colt was letting her pet him!

Christina glanced over her shoulder and smiled at the trainer. "I think he likes me," she said, slowly moving her hand over the colt's muzzle.

"Hmmm," was the only response Vince gave her.

Christina ignored him and continued to pet the colt. The grooms let their leads go slack, and Christina quickly discovered that there was a spot just behind his poll where he liked to be rubbed. She laughed when he arched his neck and curled his upper lip as she worked her fingers into his neck. "You really are a spoiled guy, aren't you?"

She turned to Vince. "I think I'm ready now," she said. "Can we take him to the track?"

"Christina!" Fredericka was coming up the aisle, smiling happily. "I'm so glad to see you, dear," Fredericka said, standing near Gratis's shoulder. The colt swung his head toward her, and his owner stroked his neck lovingly. "I see you and Gratis are getting along just fine. I'm sure you're going to be wonderful together."

Out of the corner of her eye, Christina was surprised to see Vince take off his hat and smile at Gratis's owner.

"It looks like we're set to go, Mrs. Graber," he said. Christina would never have associated that polite voice with Vince Jones. She struggled to suppress a smile.

"Wonderful," Fredericka replied, then turned back to Christina. "Are you and Gratis ready?"

Christina stood straight, looking directly at the trainer. "I think we'll be just fine," she said confidently.

"Then let's get this over with," Vince said. He took Gratis's lead line from the groom and walked the colt off.

By the time they reached the track, Christina's confidence had begun to fade. Halfway to the track, Gratis started dancing in circles, rearing up and striking at Vince, struggling to get loose. The whites of his eyes flashed as he whipped his head around, trying to bite the trainer.

Christina watched Vince circle the colt, bringing him back under control. Her heart thumped dully in her chest.

They made it to the track, and when Gratis was

somewhat settled, Vince glanced at her, then pointed at a waiting pony rider. "I'm sending you around the track the first time with an escort," he said. "The second round you'll be on your own. Do you think you can handle him?"

Christina hesitated. Gratis rolled his eyes again and flung his head up, trying to break Vince's hold on his lead.

"I'm sure of it," she said, hoping she sounded calmer than she felt. She held her hand out to Gratis, who sniffed her fingers ferociously. Then she patted his shoulder and grabbed the reins.

Vince gave her a leg up, and Gratis shifted nervously beneath her.

"It's me, boy," she said in a soft voice, stroking his shoulder. She took a deep breath, trying to make herself relax.

Vince handed the lead line to the pony rider. "Keep him at a jog," he said.

"If I can," said the pony rider—a tall, skinny boy about the same age as Christina. He was riding a palomino pony who looked unfazed by Gratis. The boy glanced up at Christina. "You're okay with this, right?" he asked.

Christina felt the colt tremble beneath her with untapped energy. "I'm fine," she said, running her hand along Gratis's shoulder in long, slow strokes. "Let's get moving." Gratis flicked his ears back when he heard her voice. "We're going to have a nice little ride, aren't we?"

"I'm just glad it's you on him, and not me," the pony rider said, turning the little palomino to lead them through the gap.

"Hold on and circle him if he gets too strong," Vince said as they moved onto the track. The colt's trembling eased and he stepped forward confidently.

"So far, so good," the boy on the pony horse said.

Christina nodded, her attention focused on Gratis's movements. She could feel his desire to break away and run, but the pony rider kept him from tearing loose.

As they moved along the rail, Gratis seemed to settle down a little more, and Christina felt the colt's incredible power as he began to stretch out. Gradually she began to sense the rhythm of his long, sweeping strides. The colt seemed to listen to her, settling his long stride almost imperceptibly. After they had finished the circuit, he was even calmer.

"He isn't so bad," her escort said. "Are you ready to go out on your own?"

Christina glanced toward the rail, where Vince was frowning in their direction. "Take him around again," the trainer called, waving his hand.

"Wish me luck," Christina said, readjusting her grip on the reins. The pony rider unclipped the lead line, and Christina started Gratis along the rail at a jog. Suddenly Gratis balked and tried to wheel around. Christina hauled on the reins in a desperate attempt to bring him back under control.

8

GRATIS CIRCLED, HUMPING HIS BACK AND SWINGING HIS hindquarters around as he pulled against the grip Christina had on the reins. He felt like an out-of-control roller coaster, heaving and surging under her. She balanced on the saddle, trying to move with the colt as he fought to break free of her hold.

"Just keep him moving!" she heard Vince call.

In a different situation Christina would have laughed. Gratis *was* moving, just not in the right direction! All Christina could think about was getting off the irate horse.

But as they spun around in another circle, she saw Vince Jones's face. The trainer's smug expression infuriated her, and she focused on her mount with new-found resolve. Gratis was not going to get the better of her.

With all the strength she had, she hauled the colt's head in the other direction, aiming his nose at the outside rail again. When she finally had him parallel to the rail, she kept a firm hand on the reins, directing him in a straight line.

"We're going around this way, boy," she said, her voice sounding a little shaky. "I'm the boss, okay?"

She felt her confidence grow as the colt settled down again, moving powerfully beneath her. For nearly a furlong things went well, and Christina started to relax a little. Then Gratis swiveled his head and tried to unseat her again. This time Christina caught him before he could turn his shoulders to follow his head. After a brief struggle, they were again going along the rail. Christina stayed alert, trying to spot any indications Gratis gave that he was about to act up again, and by the fourth time the colt tried to take control, Christina was able to stop him before he had a chance to do anything more than start to alter his gait.

She smiled to herself. "You're too predictable, boy," she said. On his fifth attempt to take control, Christina noticed the colt flick his ears to the side before he changed his stride. As they came into the second turn,

Gratis signaled with his ears, and Christina was ready. She picked up the reins and moved him away from the rail for a few steps, then steered him back. Distracted, he continued to move steadily.

By the time they finished their trip around the oval, Christina was exhausted. Gratis had made several more attempts to take off with her. She had caught him almost every time, but the one time her attention drifted slightly, he almost got his way, throwing her onto his shoulders and wheeling completely around before she could get him settled.

"Guess I can't daydream when I'm riding you, boy," she said grimly as she straightened him out. She might have discovered how to keep Gratis focused on moving forward, but it meant she couldn't let her attention slip one bit. Riding Gratis took every bit of energy she had.

She brought him to a stop where Vince and Fredericka waited at the gap, and she slipped from the colt's back with a sigh of relief. She'd done it. She'd ridden Gratis on the track and made it back in one piece.

"We can get along just fine, can't we?" she asked the colt, pausing to rub his nose. Then she looked up at the trainer and the owner. Fredericka was beaming at her, but Vince looked a little bored.

"You were fantastic," Fredericka said delightedly.

"He was a perfect angel for you!"

Christina looked down at the toes of her boots so that Gratis's owner wouldn't see the look on her face. *Angel* was the last word she would have thought of to describe Gratis.

"Not bad," Vince said. "Be here to work him at six o'clock tomorrow morning. We'll see how you manage him with a little traffic around you." He clipped Gratis's lead line to his headstall and led the horse away.

"Not bad?" Christina echoed, filled with disappointment over the backhanded compliment.

"Never mind him," Fredericka said, touching Christina's arm. "That's high praise coming from Vince. He won't say it, but he was very impressed."

"Oh." Christina felt better, but still, it would have been nice to have heard the compliment from Vince himself.

She headed for the backside, worn out from the short ride.

"Chris, wait up!"

She turned to see her mother hurrying after her. Ashleigh wrapped her arm around Christina's shoulder. "I am so proud of you," she said.

"You were watching?" Christina cocked her head at her mother. "I didn't see you."

Ashleigh grinned. "I didn't want to make you nervous."

"You wouldn't have made me nervous," Christina said.

"Yes, I would have." Ashleigh laughed. "I was so worried about your getting on that horse that I would have made it much worse for you."

"If you were so worried, why did you let me ride him?"

Ashleigh was silent for a moment as they walked past the grandstand.

"It was important to you," she said finally. "As much as I wanted to stop you, I couldn't tell you no. And you were amazing, Chris. I was so impressed." When they reached the jockey room, Ashleigh stopped. "Now hurry up and get your things so we can get some dinner."

Christina hurried off to get her from the locker room, warmed by Ashleigh's praise. It didn't matter if all Vince could say was "not bad." She had her mother's respect, and that meant a lot.

Melanie was quiet on the drive to the diner, listening silently as Christina and Ashleigh talked about their plans for the next day. The longest sentence Melanie uttered was, "I'll be there," when Ashleigh told her she wanted her to work Star first thing in the morning. After a quick burger, Ashleigh drove them back to the motel, saying good night to Melanie and Christina as she went into her own room.

Tired from her challenging ride on Gratis, Christina carried her bag into the bathroom to change and get ready for bed. When she came out of the room, Melanie was on the phone.

"If that's the way you feel, then forget it, Kevin," Melanie said, then hung up the phone.

"What's wrong?" Christina asked, but instead of answering, Melanie grabbed her jacket and stormed out the door.

Christina wondered if she should go after her, but she knew Melanie wouldn't go far. She peeked out the window and saw Melanie sitting on a bench near the motel lobby, staring up at the evening sky. She let the drape fall back, sure Melanie just needed a little time to herself.

Christina dialed the Townsend house, eager to tell Parker about her ride on Gratis.

"He sounds like a hard horse to ride," Parker said. "Are you sure he's safe?"

Christina laughed. "Just as safe as you are riding some of those cross-country courses."

"Maybe," Parker said. "But I'll still worry about you."

"Thanks, Parker," Christina said.

She was in bed by the time Melanie came back into the room. Melanie didn't say anything as she climbed into her bed. Christina rolled over to shut off the lamp.

"Is everything all right?" she asked. "Is Kevin okay?"

"Everything's fine," Melanie mumbled in response. "Good night."

In the dim light coming through the motel room window, Christina stared at the back of Melanie's blond head where it rested on the pillow. She sighed. Riding Star might not cure Melanie's seconditis, but Christina hoped it would take her cousin's mind off her problems with Kevin.

The next morning Christina made herself stand back while Melanie saddled Star. He needed to get used to Melanie handling him. "He'll be good for you," she said. "Won't you, Star?"

The colt pricked his ears at her and snorted.

"Was that a yes or a no?" Melanie asked, tightening the girth.

"It was a yes," Christina said emphatically, but she wasn't so sure. When they reached the track, June Fortig had a filly waiting for Christina. As she was settling onto the horse's back, Ashleigh pulled Melanie aside to discuss Star's workout. Christina suppressed a wave of envy and guided June's horse onto the track.

As they warmed up at a jog, she saw Melanie on Star, trotting along the outside rail ahead of them. Melanie looked stiff and uncomfortable on Star's back, and the colt kept tossing his head, trying to break into a gallop.

Christina sighed. There was nothing she could do right then. She finished working the filly with a short gallop, then brought her around to the rail, exchanging her for another of June's horses. When she got on the track again, this time on a bay colt, Melanie was cantering Star. She looked a little more comfortable, but Star's stride was short and jaunty and his head was up. Christina wanted to shout some helpful advice over to her cousin, but Melanie was too far away to hear.

By the time Christina finished working the second horse for June, Melanie and Star were off the track. Christina could see her mother leading the chestnut colt toward the backside, and Melanie was talking to Pam Mahony, who had a gray filly waiting at the side of the track. As Christina came off the track, Pam was giving Melanie a leg up onto the gray's back. Melanie gave Christina a brief wave as she rode onto the track.

At six o'clock, when Vince's handler brought Gratis out, Christina was waiting by the rail for them. The colt was alert, prancing at the end of his lead, and Christina felt a rush of excitement.

"Take him around a couple of laps at a trot," Vince said, looking from the energetic Thoroughbred to Christina.

Christina adjusted her helmet strap and nodded. Before she got on his back, she took a moment to let Gratis sniff her hands. "We're going to have a great workout, right, boy?"

She rubbed her hand down the length of his nose, then stepped to his shoulder so Vince could give her a lift onto the saddle. As she shoved her toes into the stirrups, she felt Gratis tense beneath her.

"Not like yesterday, Gratis," she said softly, petting his neck. "No tricks today, right? And no fighting."

Vince led them to the track and released the headstall, stepping back as Christina turned the colt along the rail. She picked up a slow jog, trying to keep as still as possible in the saddle.

The colt's ears flicked back and forth, and then she felt his hindquarters tense up, as though he was going to bolt. Christina adjusted her reins, making him move away from the rail and back in an effort to distract him.

"Can't you keep that horse in a straight line?" a rider yelled as he trotted by them. Gratis's ears swiveled back as the other horse passed by, and Christina felt him pick up his trot, swinging his head nervously.

"Ignore them, Gratis," Christina said. "You and I are going to be just fine."

For the next few days, working Gratis demanded all Christina's attention. On the second day she got him jogging confidently around the whole circuit, and so she asked for a canter for the last quarter mile. Gratis made the transition smoothly, but getting him back was more of a problem—she had to circle him. On the third day, Vince told her to pick up a slow gallop and go around the track twice. Gratis decided to sprint the first half mile, but Christina used her voice to get him back, and Gratis listened. They were making progress.

Christina helped Melanie get Star ready for his works, but her cousin was quiet, speaking very little, and didn't seem to be having much success with the colt. After the third day of watching Melanie struggle with Star, Christina cornered her mother at the Whitebrook stalls after the morning works.

"Mel doesn't look like she's have a good time with Star," she said. The colt hung his head over his door and nudged her gently. Christina absently toyed with his rubbery lower lip. "The way things are going, he's not going to be in any shape to race in the Futurity."

But Ashleigh shook her head. "Melanie and Star

are doing just fine," she said, sounding very sure of herself.

Christina wrinkled her nose. "But every time I see them Star's fighting her," she said.

"Trust me, Chris," Ashleigh said. "I'm not going to ruin Star's chances in the Futurity. He and Melanie are doing great."

Christina still had her doubts, but she had agreed to let Melanie exercise Star. She hoped her mother was right, that it wasn't going to hurt his chances of winning the Futurity.

By the fourth day of riding Gratis, Christina no longer had to make him weave back and forth when he started to act up. As soon as he flicked his ears to the side, she tightened the reins, and the colt moved smoothly around the track.

When she galloped him, the colt was attentive, responding to her cues perfectly, and Christina felt a rush of elation as they flew past the poles that marked the fractions. His powerful strides devoured the distance. When they had finished their gallop, Christina wanted to keep going. Instead she brought him up and headed for the rail.

Even Vince Jones was grudgingly impressed. "I think he'd be okay to race," he said as Christina handed the sweating colt off to the groom. "We'll do a six-furlong breeze tomorrow," Vince told her. "Blow his pipes out and get him ready to run. I'm going to put him in the morning draws for a race at the end of the week. Nothing big, just a chance to get him out there."

To give all the horses in any race an equal chance at a good starting position, the racing secretary held a drawing two days before the race was scheduled. At that time, too, if there were more horses entered in the race than there were gate positions, the starters were chosen by the luck of the draw.

Christina waited with eager anticipation for Vince to ask her to race Gratis for him.

"You've done a good job getting him settled," the trainer said.

Christina cracked a small smile. *Yes!* Vince had actually said she did a good job.

"I think we've got him so Steve Quinn should be able to get him through a race now," Vince said. He led Gratis toward the backside, leaving Christina speechless. All the work she had put into Gratis, and Vince was putting Steve on him?

She had only a week to convince him that *she* had to ride Gratis in his race.

9

"BRING HIM IN AFTER SIX FURLONGS," VINCE REPEATED THE next morning, holding up his stopwatch.

Christina nodded, fastening her chin strap. Behind on the track, a rider cantered by, and the sun was peeking over the eastern horizon.

A groom held Gratis, who was much more agreeable since Christina had been working him regularly. She walked to the big colt's shoulder and let him sniff her hand. Then Vince gave her a leg up, and she settled onto Gratis's back.

She guided the colt onto the track and began warming him up, trotting along the outside rail for several furlongs, then pushing him up to a canter. She could feel him straining to break loose and run, but Christina held him in. When they were beyond the starting point, she turned the colt, bringing him to the inside rail.

Then Christina leaned forward and rose off the saddle, balancing on her toes. "Come on, Gratis," she called. "Let's see what you can do!" As they galloped by the starting point, Christina felt the colt's powerful strides pick up. His fractions were getting faster and faster as he stretched out into a dead run. Each long stride covered almost twenty feet of track. Christina felt as though she were riding a rocket. The sense of speed and strength working under her was exhilarating. Too soon they passed the sixth furlong marker, and Christina began slowing the racing colt.

Gratis fought her, trying to keep moving around the track, but Christina was able to turn him, slowing him to a bouncing walk as he tried to bring his head around and take off.

"Decent" was the only comment she got from Vince Jones as she brought the colt off the track.

Christina was getting used to Vince's mannerisms, although she still thought he could be a little more personable. But she wanted Vince to be a little more enthusiastic about their performance. She'd definitely done better than Steve Quinn could do.

She worked Pam's and June's horses, then went to

see Star. She found the colt in his stall, tearing bites of hay from the full net hanging from the wall. Maureen Mack, Whitebrook's assistant trainer, was sitting in front of the stalls, reading a copy of the *Daily Racing Form.*

"Have you seen Mom and Melanie?" Christina asked. She had caught a glimpse of her mother and cousin at the track earlier, but she had been so busy with Gratis that she hadn't had time to watch Star's workout.

"They went over to Vince Jones's barn," Maureen replied, glancing up from her paper. "Fredericka Graber came by to see Star, and she told your mother she was thinking about selling that Townsend filly she has. So your mom and Mel went over to look at her."

"Oh." Christina had been wanting to take Melanie to see Image herself. But Melanie had probably forgotten all about it. She seemed a little distracted lately.

"How was Star's workout today?" Christina asked.

Maureen set the paper aside and smiled at Christina. "He and Melanie are looking better together every day," she said.

"That's good," Christina replied, leaning against Star's stall door. The colt shoved his nose in her direction, then went back to eating his hay. *But I would rather have heard it from Melanie,* Christina thought.

By the afternoon, Christina still hadn't seen Melanie. She walked through the jockey room before the races, looking for her.

"Hey, Reese," Steve called from where he was sitting with George and a few other jockeys Christina didn't care for. "Thanks for getting that Vince Jones colt ready for me to race." He laughed loudly, and George and Raoul Menendez joined in. "Vince said to let you know he won't need you tomorrow. He wants to colt to lay off for a day before I race him."

Christina worked her jaw, longing to snap some witty response at Steve, but nothing came out. Where was Melanie when she needed her most? Her cousin would have had some quick retort that would have shut Steve up. Christina hurried away from the laughing group, fuming at herself for being so slow.

The next morning she had time to watch Melanie work Star. They did three laps of the track at a nice, easy canter. Star's stride was low and long, and Melanie was quiet on his back, following his stride perfectly, moving as one with the cantering horse. Christina had to admit her cousin looked good on the colt, and Star seemed to have settled down.

"I'm going to have Melanie breeze him in a couple of days," Ashleigh told Christina. "We'll compare the time to what you've done on him, and then we'll lay him off until the Futurity."

Christina nodded. But as much as she wanted to see Star and Melanie do well, she still liked the idea that the colt would give that little extra something just for her.

That afternoon Christina was waiting by the viewing paddock when Gratis was brought up for his race. A woman handler she hadn't seen before led the colt to the saddling ring. Christina was pleased to see that he seemed to be behaving himself.

"That's a good boy," Christina murmured to herself. Maybe Steve would pull it off, and she'd have to admit she hadn't given him enough credit. For Gratis's sake, she hoped the colt would behave himself. Steve was wearing Fredericka Graber's purple-and-green silks, waiting beside Gratis's owner as the horses were brought around the ring.

When it was time for the jockey to mount up, however, Gratis pressed his ears back and lunged his hips away, trying to keep Steve from getting on his back. Despite the colt's efforts, the jockey was soon on board. Moments later Gratis was being ponied down the track with the rest of the racehorses.

Christina watched, dismayed, as the powerful bay horse minced and bucked, trying to dislodge his rider and kick the pony horse. She hoped they would make it to the gate without a horse getting injured. But even if they did get there without a major incident, Gratis was going to wear himself out before the race even started.

"He doesn't look good, does he?"

Christina glanced up as Fredericka Graber rested her hands on the rail and frowned in the direction of the parading horses.

"I hope he's okay," Christina replied. "He seems so upset."

"Vince assured me Steve is a very good jockey," Fredericka said. "He'll do fine, I'm sure."

But Gratis balked the whole way down the track. There was a struggle at the back of the gate as the crew tried to load him into his chute. Christina ground her teeth as the minutes passed. The horses already loaded in their chutes were growing impatient, but even behind the gate, Gratis bucked and reared, striking at the gate crew.

A track van sped over to the starting gate and one of the track veterinarians climbed from the vehicle. Christina knew it was normal for the vet to check a horse in this kind of situation. Often a struggling horse got nicked or bumped, and the trainer only wanted to make sure it was sound to race. But she held her breath, hoping there was nothing seriously wrong with the colt.

Finally the announcer's voice came over the loud-speakers. "Number seven, Gratis, has been pulled from the race." Christina gasped, and Fredericka clutched her elbow. Moments later the starting bell sounded and the race began. Gratis was held back behind the gate.

Christina paid no attention to the race. She and Fredericka stood side by side, eyes fixed on the gate, waiting silently for it to end. As soon as it was over, Gratis was led off the track by a pony rider, still dancing and fighting at the end of the lead line. Fredericka Christina hurried toward the backside to be there when Gratis returned to the stable.

When they reached the barn, Gratis's handler was walking the colt in circles, trying to calm him down, and Steve Quinn was storming back to the men's locker room, a dark look on his face. He brushed past Christina, mumbling about spoiled, worthless horses as he went.

Christina ignored the jockey and headed straight for the aggravated colt. "Hey, grumpy," she said. "What's wrong, silly boy?"

At the sound of her voice, the colt flicked his ears in her direction. Then he trumpeted angrily and struck at the ground with a powerful hoof.

"Quit acting like such a jerk," Christina said, raising her hand so he could sniff her fingers. Gratis snorted loudly and whooshed out a loud breath.

"That's more like it," she said, taking a step closer to him. Gratis angled his head and looked down at her. Christina stood still, waiting for him to bring his head down. Finally he rested his muzzle lightly on her shoulder, and Christina stroked his nose tenderly.

Vince was striding down the aisle, a look of disgust on his face. He glared at Gratis, shaking his head. "That horse is a waste of time," he grumbled, stalking into his office.

Fredericka followed him in. "*Now* will you listen to me, Vince?" Christina heard her say. Vince's reply was sharp, but Christina couldn't make out the words. Was he going to try to convince Fredericka to sell Gratis? Christina strained her ears to hear what they were saying, but their voices were muffled. She gave up and turned her attention back to Gratis.

"Thanks for your help," the groom said. "Vince told me I shouldn't have any trouble with him because I'm a woman, but I don't think I could have handled him without your help."

"He's just a big dope," Christina said affectionately. She gave Gratis's sweaty shoulder a quick pat.

"I'd better go cool him out," the groom said, shaking her head. "He's so hot, you'd think he did run that race."

She led the colt away, and Christina headed back to the track.

Suddenly Vince stuck his head out his office door. "You," he barked, pointing at Christina. "Come here."

Christina hesitated a moment before she approached the trainer.

"What's your little trick for handling that colt?" Vince asked, pinning her with his eyes. "You've got some trick, I know you do."

"I don't have any tricks," Christina said quickly. "I just listen to him, that's all."

Vince pulled his hat off and rubbed his hand across his forehead. "I still need to get that colt in a race while he's here." He narrowed his eyes at her again. "You're sure you don't have some little secret you could tell me? I've got to find some jockey who can ride him in a race."

"I'm a jockey," Christina reminded him, folding her arms across her chest.

Vince gave her a sour look. "I guess I could have you on him in a race. You're not my first choice, but I'm getting desperate."

Christina bit her lip. Having Vince ask her to ride for him wasn't quite as flattering as she had imagined it would be. "Don't forget," she reminded him, "I'm only a bug."

Vince winced and shook his head. "A bug," he repeated, then sighed deeply. "I never use bugs."

"Then I guess you don't want me," Christina said, turning away.

"I don't think I have a choice at this point," Vince said. "If he's going to run, you'll have to ride him."

"Are you sure?" Christina asked.

"No," Vince said dryly. "I'm not sure. Do you want the job or not?"

Christina paused.

"Is it that hard?" Vince asked impatiently. "Either you're going to do it or you're not."

Christina's attention drifted to where Gratis's handler was walking him up and down in front of the shedrows. His bay coat glistened in the afternoon sun. The colt was such a character, and so misunderstood. She couldn't bear to watch him fight with another jockey and be denied the chance to run. More than that, she couldn't bear to see Fredericka give in and sell him because no one would ride him.

"Yes," she said. "I'll do it." Thanks to Gratis, Vince Jones was offering her a chance. She had to take it.

"Fine," Vince said, walking back into his office. He sat down behind his desk, then glanced up at Christina again. "I'll put him in the morning draws on Monday, and we'll get him in a race."

Christina hurried to the locker room. She didn't see Melanie when she went into the locker room, but when she came back into the jockey room, Steve was waiting for her.

"Nice going, bug," he said. "You're really going to show me up, aren't you?"

Christina stared at him. "I don't know what you're talking about."

"That bay colt," Steve said, folding his arms across his chest. "I went back to Vince to let him know I'd try the colt again, and he told me he was putting you on him for his next race. You'll find out you're not such a hotshot when you get him out there in a race."

Christina bristled. "I've been handling him just fine," she said, glowering at the jockey.

"The colt may be fine for you when the track is empty, but he'll flip when he gets charged up with race-day tension. And you don't have the experience to handle it." Steve turned abruptly and stalked off.

Christina heard someone behind her and turned to find Melanie staring at her.

"Can you believe that guy?" she demanded. If her cousin had been right there, she must have heard what Steve said. But why hadn't she said anything in Christina's defense?

Melanie shrugged. "I think he may be right," she

said. "There are a lot of more experienced jockeys Vince could get for Gratis. You could get into a lot of trouble on a horse like that."

Christina watched in hurt amazement as Melanie headed for the showers. Then she sank down on a chair and rested her chin on her hands. Was Melanie just repeating Steve's words, or was she right? Was Gratis too much horse for her to manage?

10

TWO DAYS LATER VINCE BROUGHT GRATIS BACK OUT TO THE track. Christina watched the colt mincing and bucking all the way to the gap, with Vince circling him every few steps, trying to keep him under control.

When Christina settled onto his back, she felt the tension humming in him, and she sighed, stroking his shoulder.

"You're not going to give me a break, are you?" she asked him. Gratis swiveled his ears back at the sound of her voice, but as Vince unclipped the lead line, the colt lunged away from him and onto the track.

Christina hauled on the reins, stopping Gratis before he could turn the morning workout into a rodeo ride. But it took every bit of skill she had to get him moving along the rail.

"Isn't this where we started last week, boy?" she asked, tightening the reins and watching for the telltale signs that the colt was going to bolt with her.

They broke into a tight, bouncy trot. With gentle hands, Christina followed the movement of Gratis's head, gradually relaxing the pressure on the reins until he dropped his head and lengthened his stride.

Near the end of the workout, Gratis was quiet and responsive, but Christina didn't dare let down her guard, just in case he decided to test her one more time.

When they came off the track, Gratis's neck was glistening with sweat. Christina wondered if he felt as exhausted as she did. Vince handed the colt to a handler, who draped one of Fredericka Graber's purple-and-green sheets over the colt's steaming back and led the now quiet horse away from the track. Christina thought longingly of the locker room, where she could take a long, soothing shower. She was glad that Gratis was her last horse of the morning.

But today Melanie was going to breeze Star, and she didn't want to miss seeing her colt work.

Farther down the track, she saw her mother leading Star to the track, with Melanie at her side. She hurried to meet them, giving her mother and cousin a quick smile before running her hand along Star's neck.

"You're going to be good for Melanie, aren't you,

boy?" she said, cupping the colt's smooth jaw with her hands. Star snuffled at the front of her shirt, making Christina laugh. "I don't have any treats for you, greedy. You have to work before you can eat." She turned to Melanie, but her cousin was checking Star's girth and didn't look at her.

"Ready?" Ashleigh said, offering Melanie a leg up.

Christina stepped back, trying not to feel a little envious when she saw how good her cousin looked on the chestnut colt. Ashleigh unclipped the lead, and Melanie headed Star onto the track, warming him up along the outside rail. Star looked alert and focused, although Christina could tell Melanie was working hard to keep him that way. By the time the pair passed by again, Star was galloping long and low, his neck stretched out, his legs reaching their full extension, while his hooves ate up the dirt.

"They're doing just fine, Chris," Ashleigh said, joining her at the rail.

Christina had to agree. She hadn't seen Star go this well . . . *ever*. But she hoped he looked equally amazing when she was on his back.

Ashleigh lifted her stopwatch, and Christina held her breath, watching her beautiful colt fly along the track as though he had winged feet. Her heart was with him every step of the way, and when Melanie brought him up at the end of the fifth furlong, Christina felt as though she had been running beside them.

She darted a look at her mother, who was staring at the stopwatch.

"Well?" she demanded. "How did they do?"

"An eighth of a second off your last five-furlong breeze," Ashleigh replied.

Christina hesitated for a moment. "Slower, right?"

But Ashleigh was shaking her head. "Faster."

Christina caught her breath. Star had run faster for Melanie. She forced a bright smile to her face. "Good," she said. "That means he's getting better every day. Imagine what he'll be like as a three-year-old. He'll be untouchable!"

Ashleigh smiled. "Yes, that's right," she said as Melanie brought Star off the track. "I'm glad you can see this is no reflection on your riding, Chris. Star *is* getting better every day, and I'm sure he'll run just as fast for you in the Futurity. Or even faster."

Melanie's face was animated, her eyes bright. "Did you see that?" she asked Christina as she jumped from Star's back. "He was amazing, wasn't he?" She looked happier than she had in days.

Christina nodded in agreement. "Amazing," she said, petting Star's steaming neck.

"Go put him up," Ashleigh told Christina and

Melanie. "Then hurry up and shower if you want to go to the morning draws with me."

"Definitely. Just as soon as I give Star a nice warm bubble bath," Christina said. "And we're going to draw a great rail position for the Futurity, right, boy?" she asked the colt, rubbing his nose.

Melanie shrugged. "I don't need to go to the draw. I'll take care of Star if you want, Chris," she offered.

"That's all right, I can do it," Christina countered. "I haven't spent much time with him in the last few days. I miss him."

After she cooled Star out and bathed him, Christina hurried to the locker room. She showered quickly and dressed, then made her way to Whitebrook's stabling area to meet her mother.

Ashleigh and Maureen were sitting in front of the stalls, going over a copy of Turfway's condition book, the program that showed all the track's scheduled races for the year.

Ashleigh handed the booklet to Maureen. "If Star doesn't make the draw for the Futurity, I don't see any other races I want to enter him in here. If he doesn't run in the Futurity, I guess we'll just have to wait until Keeneland to run him."

Christina paused in front of Star's stall. The colt hung his head over the door and bumped her with his nose. "He'll make the draw, Mom," she said. "He has to." She rubbed Star's forehead. "We're going to put you in a race, Star," she told him. "Isn't that exciting?"

The colt nuzzled her shirt, and Christina dug in her pocket for the apple she had brought him. Star crunched it happily while Christina leaned against his stall door.

"Let's get going," Ashleigh said finally, standing up. "It's almost eleven. We're going to be stuck in the back of the room for the draw as it is."

As they crossed the grounds toward the racing secretary's office, Christina's mind was filled with excitement about the race. The Futurity was going to be her biggest race yet, and she was confident she and Star stood a good chance of winning it, especially after Star's excellent time that morning and all her practice on Gratis.

She followed Ashleigh into the crowded lobby of the racing secretary's office, squeezing into a corner beside a pair of jockeys' agents and some trainers she didn't know. Across the room, she saw Tommy Turner with his agent. The other jockey waved, then turned his attention to the front of the room. The draws, a daily ritual at the track, were the process by which horses and gate positions were selected for the races scheduled two days later.

The racing commission was allowing a field of ten for this year's Futurity. Since the Breeder's Futurity was a popular race, Christina knew there would be more horses than gate positions entered in the draw. Two lists would be created from the drawing. The first list would have only as many names on it as there were starting gates. The second list would be those horses who weren't drawn in the first ten. If Star only made it onto the second list, he couldn't race unless one of the first picks was scratched. And even then it would depend on how far down the second list he was drawn. Christina crossed her fingers. This race was too important for Star not to run in it. She didn't want to wait until Keeneland to race him again.

Christina stood on tiptoe, peering between the backs of agents', trainers', and owners' heads to see the front of the room. She caught a glimpse of a conference table, where a big wire tumbler full of white chips sat. Christina knew each chip was numbered with a gate position. As she watched, the secretary and his assistant started the process of setting up the scheduled races.

The trainers and agents crowded near the table, making notes on their horses and jockeys. Christina saw Vince Jones near the front of the crowd, but there were so many people between them that she couldn't get to the trainer to ask which horses he was entering in the day's draws. With ten races scheduled for Sunday, he could have several horses running. A smile tugged at the corners of her mouth. Wouldn't it be something if she was able to ride Gratis and Star on the same day? And win on both of them!

The scattered conversations that filled the room lowered to a murmur as the racing secretary took his position behind the table. A tall, thin man dressed in a suit and tie, the racing secretary had a bald head that gleamed under the harsh overhead lights. He raised his arm and the room fell silent.

The secretary's assistant was no older than twenty and very short and stout, like a jockey who'd overeaten. He wore a blue suit and stood beside the secretary, looking self-important with a clipboard in one hand and a pen tucked behind his ear.

The secretary and his assistant began the long process of going through the lists of the claiming races to be run on Sunday, then one stakes race. Christina only half listened, waiting impatiently to hear how the Futurity would be drawn. After each race was called, agents shoved their way through the crowded room, trying to be the first to reach the trainers whose horses didn't have jockeys named to ride them.

Ashleigh shook her head. "I hate this part of racing," she said. "All the agents fighting to get rides for their jockeys, and trainers arguing with the secretary over how a race has been drawn." She and Christina stayed out of the fray, keeping to the back wall.

"This is for the Breeder's Futurity," the assistant finally said in a loud voice, speaking over the low roar of voices that filled the room after the latest race had been called. Most of the talk quieted as the trainers and agents turned their attention back to the front of the room.

The assistant cleared his throat. "This is a mile and an eighth, a grade two stakes race for two-year-old colts."

He began pulling the names of the horses whose trainers had entered them for the race.

"Like the Wind," he said loudly. "No jockey."

The secretary spun the tumbler and reached inside. "Gate two," he called.

When the agents in the room heard that Like the Wind was riderless, they swarmed toward the colt's trainer. Christina wrinkled her nose as several agents shoved through the crowded room, waving their arms and yelling the names of jockeys they represented.

After a minute the hubbub faded, and the assistant grabbed another slip of paper. "Rockafella, Greg Fryhling, jockey," the assistant intoned. The secretary called gate nine for Rockafella.

Christina wrinkled her nose. Greg was nice, but he was a very aggressive rider. She and Star would have to be careful of him.

The first and seventh gate positions were called, and Christina held her breath, waiting for Star's name to be called.

"Sunny Gold," the assistant said. "Tommy Turner riding."

Tommy's ride drew gate eight. Christina tapped her foot impatiently, afraid that Star might not get into the race after all.

The assistant glanced down at his list again. "Wonder's Star, with Christina Reese riding," the assistant said.

The racing secretary reached into the tumbler and pulled out a chip. "Gate number three," he announced, setting Star's gate position.

Christina was elated. Star was in the race, and they had drawn an excellent starting position. She imagined them in the gate, waiting for the starting bell. She could feel the colt shifting beneath her, eager to run.

"This is going to be a great race," she murmured to Ashleigh, who looked pleased about Star's luck in the draw.

Ashleigh nodded. "You have a good gate position, and I know Star is in prime condition for this race.

Now be quiet so we can hear which horses are going to fill the field."

The assistant's voice rang out again. "Dragonfly, Steve Quinn riding."

"Gate four," the secretary announced.

Christina winced. Steve would be beside her. She'd just have to deal with it, she decided. She wouldn't let him bother her.

Then the assistant held up another piece of paper. "Gratis," he said loudly. "Christina Reese riding."

"Number five," the secretary said, but Christina barely heard the colt's position number.

Her mind reeled. She didn't hear the last two positions being called as the assistant's words echoed in her head. Star and Gratis were in the same race—and she'd been named to ride both of them!

11

"WHAT AM I GOING TO DO?" CHRISTINA SAID DESPERATELY, turning to her mother.

"Obviously you have to pick between Star and Gratis," Ashleigh said calmly. "That's not much of a decision, is it? You'll ride Star, of course."

People moved past them, heading out the door. The racing secretary and his assistant began picking up the tumbler and the lists. Christina felt her shoulders sag. Her mother didn't seem to understand that choosing between Star and Gratis wasn't as simple as she made it sound.

Vince Jones was making his way through the crowd, but he didn't notice Ashleigh and Christina as he left the lobby. Christina thought of Gratis. She had figured out how to make the colt work for her. Now Vince was giving her the chance to show him, and everyone else, that she could handle a race on Gratis.

But Star needed her. The Futurity could make a difference in his standing in upcoming races, and she couldn't take that away from him. She gave a soft groan and pressed her hands to her face. "I don't know what to do," she said into her palms.

"I can't help you decide, Chris," Ashleigh said. "Obviously I'd prefer to have you ride Star. From what I've seen, Gratis is unpredictable and dangerous. I know you can handle exercising him, but I don't want to see you risking yourself in a race with that colt."

"But I understand him, Mom," Christina protested. "He listens to me."

Ashleigh gazed at her steadily. "Do you realize what you're saying, Chris? You're really picking Gratis over Star?"

Christina dropped her gaze, an image of Star burning in her mind's eye. She saw her majestic colt dashing exuberantly across his paddock at Whitebrook, and she shook her head. "I can't desert Star," she said.

Ashleigh frowned, rubbing her fingertips across her forehead. "I won't force you to ride Star, Chris. It's up to you to decide."

"I can't," Christina said, dropping her hands to her sides.

"You'd better make up your mind quickly," Ashleigh said. "If you're riding Star, you have to let Vince know. He'll need to find another jockey, if he can. And if you're riding Gratis, I'll need to pull Star out of the race."

"Pull Star?" Christina gave her mother a horrified look. "You can't! This is a big race for him."

"I know," Ashleigh said. "But I can't race him without a jockey."

"What about you?" Christina asked. "You handled him great at Ellis Park. Couldn't you do it again?"

Ashleigh shook her head. "I promised your father I wouldn't. It would be very easy to keep racing 'just one more time.' I'd like to, Chris, but I can't fix this for you."

"I know, Mom." Christina groaned. "This is my chance to ride someone else's horse against a field of really good Thoroughbreds. But Star . . ." Her voice faded away.

"What about Star?" Ashleigh asked quietly.

"You can't scratch him, Mom," Christina said. "He deserves a chance to run in this race, too."

Ashleigh tilted her head and eyed Christina. "But he needs you to do it."

Christina hesitated. Star did need her. Or did he? She thought of Melanie's breeze on the colt earlier. He had run beautifully for her.

Was she selling him short? Maybe she was just afraid to see him do well without her. Or maybe she was afraid she wouldn't do well without him.

"I need to talk to Maureen about Star's schedule until the race," Ashleigh said. "I'll see you at his stall. You can let me know what you've decided then."

Christina exhaled and dropped her chin. If she could get a win out of Gratis in the Futurity, she'd gain a lot of respect in the racing world. But after everything she and Star had been through together, how could she turn away from him?

Christina watched her mother walk away. Was she fooling herself, thinking she could manage a colt as unpredictable as Gratis against a field of first-class racehorses and top-notch jockeys? She needed to talk to someone who wouldn't pressure her. She walked out of the racing secretary's office, stopping at the pay phone near the door. She needed to talk to Parker.

She dialed the Townsend house, and to her relief, Parker answered the phone. She quickly filled him in on her dilemma.

There was a long silence, then she heard her boyfriend sigh. "I know you probably don't want to hear the Brad Townsend school of thought," he said, "but my dad always says to weigh your risks, then take the one with the largest payoff."

"The trouble is," Christina said, "I have to think of what's going to be best for Star, too."

"I need to go," Parker said. "I'm helping Sam teach a jumping class this afternoon, and I'm already late."

"Thanks for listening to me, Parker," Christina said. "Give Sterling a pat for me, okay?"

"Sure," Parker said.

Christina hung up the phone and headed for Vince's stable, slowing when she saw Fredericka Graber striding toward her.

"Christina, I'm so glad I found you!" Fredericka said when she reached her. "Vince told me about the draw. This is a terrible problem, isn't it?"

Christina nodded, unable to think of anything to say.

Fredericka didn't seem to notice. She reached out to catch one of Christina's hands, clasping it in hers. "I've been counting on you to ride him in the race because he goes so wonderfully for you," she said earnestly. "I'm afraid that if you don't, Vince is going to give up on him. One more catastrophe like our last race, and he won't want to put any more training into him. I don't know if I could find another trainer who could take what Gratis has put Vince through. And I . . . I might have to sell him."

"No!" Christina said.

Fredericka smiled sadly. "Not everyone has the right touch, Christina. You have something special with Gratis. Please say you'll ride him. For me."

Christina felt as though she was being pulled in two directions. Fredericka didn't know how attached Christina was to Star and that she had something even more special with him. She didn't want to turn her back on Star, but if it hadn't been for Fredericka, she was sure Vince never would have given her a chance to ride Gratis in the first place. She couldn't refuse Gratis's owner after all the support and praise Fredericka had given her.

She forced a smile. "I'll ride Gratis," she said. "Right now, though, I need to go talk to my mom about Star."

"Thank you so much," Fredericka said. "I'll let Vince know." She hurried back toward the trainer's stables, and Christina headed for the Whitebrook stalls to let her mother know she wouldn't be riding Star.

When she neared Star's stall, the colt stuck his head over his door and whinnied at her. Glad for the distraction, she paused to rub his neck. Star playfully lipped at her hair, curling his lip at the taste of her shampoo. Christina laughed, rubbing his upper lip with her fingertips.

"You are the greatest horse in the world, aren't you?"

Star exhaled noisily, and Christina massaged his poll. "Could you run a race for someone else now, Star? Would you run for Melanie?" Star nudged her, and she resumed petting him. "You deserve a chance to prove yourself, too, don't you, boy?" she asked. "Otherwise everyone will say you're strictly a one-person horse. I know you're better than that. You'll run because it's what you were bred to do, not just because it's me asking you to."

Christina let her hand go still, and Star shoved at it. She wrapped her arms around his neck and sighed. "I love you, Star."

Christina heard her mother's and Maureen's voices as the trainers came up the aisle. Maureen walked into Rascal's stall, and Ashleigh gazed at Christina expectantly.

Christina eyed Star, then looked at her mother. "What about Melanie?" she asked. "Melanie beat my last work time on him. He might come through for her in a race, too."

Ashleigh frowned thoughtfully and bit her lip. "I wanted to wait a bit before putting Mel in a race—let her get her confidence back. But they have been pulling together nicely," she agreed. "Maybe you're right. Star looks like he'd go well for her. You think Melanie would do it?"

"I'll go talk to her," Christina said. "I'm sure she'll jump at the chance."

"If Mel will do it, that's fine," Ashleigh said.

"Thanks, Mom," Christina said. "I wish I could ride Star, but Melanie will do a great job. I'm sure of it."

"She's probably in the locker room if you want to go talk to her," Ashleigh said.

Christina hurried off in search of Melanie. She found her in the jockey room, watching simulcast races with Vicky Frontiere.

"Mel, can I talk to you?" Christina asked.

Melanie's gaze flicked back to the television, then slowly she rose and followed Christina into the locker room. "What's up?" she asked as Christina turned to face her.

Melanie's unsmiling face worried Christina. But she was sure offering Melanie the chance to race Star would boost her cousin's spirits.

"How would you like to ride a really good horse in a really good race?" she asked.

"What are you talking about?" Melanie asked, frowning suspiciously.

"Star in the Breeder's Futurity," Christina said. "Gratis and Star are in the same race. I'm going to ride Gratis, and you can ride Star. Please, Melanie, say yes."

Melanie sank onto one of the benches lining the wall and looked up at Christina with a sad expression. "I can't," she said.

"What do you mean, you can't?" Christina stared at her cousin in dismay.

"I'm sorry, Chris," Melanie said. "If I thought I could do it, of course I'd ride Star for you, but I just can't. I may be a decent exercise rider, but I just don't cut it as a jockey. You don't want Star to lose, do you?"

Christina stared at Melanie. "Oh, Mel, what are you saying?"

Melanie's chin quivered, and tears began trickling down her face. "I called Kevin to tell him about breezing Star," she said, her voice breaking. "I was so excited about the work. It was the best I've felt about riding in ages."

"You looked fantastic," Christina agreed. "I don't understand. Why are you so upset?"

"Kevin broke up with me," Melanie sobbed. "He says I'm obsessed with trying to win a race, and I'm no fun anymore. He said I'm letting racing take over my life, and he doesn't want to be around me." Melanie's shoulders started to shake as she buried her face in her

139

hands. "He's right," she mumbled. "I'm a lousy jockey. I can't take Star into the Futurity. I'd ruin it for him."

"That's not true. You're a good jockey, Mel," Christina said reassuringly. She wrapped her arm around Melanie's shoulder. "Kevin's wrong. He's just jealous of the time you spend on the track. Don't listen to him. So you've had a few weeks of bad luck. So what? Before that you were doing great, and since you've been working with Star, you're back on top again."

"I've ridden one race since I started working Star, Chris. And I didn't win. Again."

"But you almost did," Christina argued. "You *practically* won."

Melanie folded her arms over her chest and shook her head. "Sorry, Chris. I don't think Star was the magic cure for seconditis after all."

"I don't know," Christina countered. "Maybe you should race him to find out."

Melanie swiped at her tear-streaked face. Her blue eyes were bloodshot and sad. "The Futurity is a big deal, Chris. At this point I really think I should stick to the smaller ones. I'm sorry, but I can't race him for you."

12

"It's okay, Mel. I understand," Christina said slowly. "I'm sorry about you and Kevin, Mel. And don't worry—Mom and I will figure something out for Star."

She left the locker room to track her mother down. She found her at the Whitebrook stalls, talking to Maureen.

When Christina gave her the news about Melanie, Ashleigh looked unhappy. "Well, no one can make her do it. I certainly don't want to push her," she said. "I think she's ready. But until *she* thinks she's ready, she's not really ready."

"I'm sorry, Mom," Christina said sadly. It broke her heart to be letting Star and her family down. She wanted to feel good about her choice to ride Gratis, but just then it didn't feel like the right choice. Not at all.

"We can put off scratching Star until Sunday morning," Ashleigh said. "Maybe you'll change your mind."

But Christina couldn't switch horses now. She was committed to ride Gratis. She only hoped she could make this up to Star when they got to Keeneland.

She clung to the hope Melanie would have a change of heart, but by the time they returned to their motel room Friday evening, Melanie was still withdrawn and teary.

When they arrived at Turfway Saturday morning, the sun was just breaking the horizon as Christina headed for the track. Vince was keeping Gratis in his stall until the race the next day, and Ashleigh was acting as though Star was still going to race, keeping him stalled for the day, too.

When she reached the track, Christina spotted Pam Mahony standing near the gap with Decisive Moment, the first horse Christina was scheduled to work that morning. "I want you to give him a two-mile gallop this morning," the trainer said, offering Christina a leg up onto the colt's back. "I want him in perfect form for the Kentucky Cup next Saturday." Pam held the colt's head while Christina found her stirrups and collected the reins.

"It's going to be a great race," Christina said as Pam released the lead shank.

Christina could see Melanie, already working a bay colt on the track. She warmed up Decisive Moment at a brisk trot, then pushed him to a gallop, enjoying the feel of the powerful horse working beneath her as they circled the track.

When she brought the colt to a stop near the opening in the rail, she saw Vince Jones watching her.

After Christina turned Dee over to his trainer, Vince approached her, a deep frown on his face. "Mrs. Graber is determined that you're going to ride Gratis tomorrow," he said. "But I don't think it's in the horse's best interest or Mrs. Graber's. I really don't think you can handle it."

"Handle what?" Christina asked. "Gratis has been going really well for me. I'm not afraid to ride him."

"I'm not worried about that," Vince said, scowling at her. "I'm afraid you'll be biased toward your own colt, that you won't ride Gratis to his best because of Star."

"It won't be a problem," Christina said. It would be easy, in fact, since Star wasn't racing.

"You sound pretty sure of yourself," Vince replied. "How do I know you can deal with racing against your own horse?"

Christina pressed her lips together and looked at Vince steadily. "Because we're pulling Star out of the race," she said. "I won't be riding against him."

The look Vince gave her was pure amazement. "You're pulling Wonder's Star?" A frown creased his brow. "Why?"

Christina quickly told him about Melanie's fear that she would ruin the race for Star. She winced as Vince's scowl deepened. He didn't care about her cousin's problems—why was she confiding in Vince, of all people? *Act professional*, Christina reminded herself.

"I guess I'll leave you on Gratis, then," Vince said, as if he wished things were otherwise. Just then Christina's next horse was brought up for her to work, and Vince walked away without another word to her.

That evening in the motel room, Melanie was quiet, her attention on a novel she had picked up in the lobby.

Christina tried to watch a TV show with the sound turned way down, but her mind kept wandering to the next day's race. She wished she could convince Melanie to reconsider racing Star, but she didn't want to be too pushy. Finally she shut off the television and climbed under the covers.

Just then Melanie set her book aside. "I went over to see that black filly at Vince Jones's barn again," she said.

Christina glanced up and smiled. "Image? She's so cute, isn't she?"

Melanie nodded. "Vince came by while I was looking at her."

"Oh?" Christina waited, sensing that Melanie had more to say.

"He said he's been watching me work on the track in the mornings," she said, a smile playing at the corners of her mouth. "He said I'm a pretty decent rider."

Christina laughed. "That's like the best praise you could get from Vince," she said.

"Then he just glared at me and asked if I was a quitter," Melanie said. "He told me that if I had a chance to ride in the Futurity, I'd be a fool not to take it. That's what he called me, a fool."

"What did you tell him?" Christina asked, then held her breath.

"That I'm no quitter, of course," Melanie said, folding her arms across her chest and flashing the feisty grin that Christina hadn't seen in a long, long time.

"Does this mean that you'll ride Star?" Christina had to restrain herself from jumping off her bed.

Melanie nodded. "I have to try," she said. "I can't just give up on racing. Besides, I can't let you guys scratch him because I won't ride him."

"Oh, thank you, Mel! We have to tell Mom!"

Christina exclaimed. "She'll be so relieved."

"She already knows," Melanie said. "I wanted to tell you myself, but I kept putting it off this afternoon. I was afraid you'd be upset with me."

"Why?" Christina asked.

"Because I've been acting like such an idiot," Melanie said. "Do you still want me to ride him?"

"Of course I do!" Christina said. "I know you can handle him. This is so great, Mel."

Melanie flashed her a cocky grin. "Just don't be mad if we win."

"I'm so nervous, my hands won't stop shaking," Melanie said, fumbling with the chin strap on her helmet. "What about you, Chris?"

Christina forced herself to smile at Melanie as they strode toward the viewing paddock. Fans were starting to gather around the paddock fence.

"I'm scared to death," she said, pulling her helmet on. "This is going to be a weird race, I can feel it. I've got shivers."

"I know," Melanie said. "This makes no sense, but I've never ridden against someone that I want to see win. I mean, I want to win, too."

"Exactly," Christina said as they walked into the

146

paddock. She flashed a tight smile at Melanie. "Good luck, Mel."

"You too," Melanie said, heading to where Ashleigh was waiting at the number three position, holding Star between them. The colt's copper coat was gleaming, and he looked alert and ready to go.

Christina hesitated for a moment, gazing across the paddock at her mother and Star. It felt so strange not to walk right up to them, mount up, and wait for Ashleigh's instructions. Ashleigh waved to her and mouthed, "Good luck." Christina smiled and waved back, then turned away, heading for the number five spot, where Fredericka was waiting for her. Vince hadn't brought Gratis up from the backside yet.

"I'm looking forward to this race, Christina," Fredericka said, looking like the wealthy horse owner she was, in her deep purple silk skirt and jacket, the brilliant emeralds in her necklace and earrings reflecting the afternoon sun. "No matter how things go today, I am glad it's you riding my Gratis."

"Thank you," Christina said, smoothing her hands down the front of her green-and-purple racing shirt. She gave Fredericka a tense smile. "Thank you for giving me the chance to ride him. I hope we do okay out there."

The colt's owner gave her a confident nod. "Gratis

will be perfect for you today, Christina. I'm certain of it."

"I sure hope so," Christina said nervously.

"Hey, Chris!"

Parker's voice drew her attention to the paddock fence. She looked up to see Parker and Kevin waving at her, and she waved back, smiling at her boyfriend.

Kevin looked toward Melanie and called her name. When Melanie looked in his direction, Kevin gave her a thumbs-up. "Good luck," he called. "I'll be cheering for you."

To Christina's relief, Melanie gave him a confident smile.

As the handlers began parading the horses around the paddock, Christina's attention turned to the horses.

She examined the first two horses as they pranced by, looking fit and sleek. Unconditional, the number one horse, was a handsome dark-brown colt. He minced around the paddock, fighting his handler every step of the way. The number two horse, Like the Wind, was calmer, alert, and poised.

Then Dani led Star past her, the number three blanket draped across his back. The colt swung his head in Christina's direction as he caught her scent. Christina clenched her fists at her sides, resisting the urge to reach out to her handsome chestnut colt. Star fought the groom's hold on his lead, trying to walk toward Christina. Dani gave a tug on his lead, but Star stomped and snorted.

"It's all right, Star," Christina whispered under her breath. Finally Dani got him moving again, but as they walked away, Star angled his head back at Christina, and he whinnied long and loud.

Christina felt on the verge of tears. What was she doing? Star was the horse she wanted to be on. She and Star were a team. This was a huge mistake.

The number four horse, Dragonfly, looked magnificent. He was a striking bay colt with a single white stocking on his off foreleg. He walked past them calmly, but in his eye was a determined look that made Christina's heart speed up.

When Vince's groom stopped Gratis in front of her, Christina admired the awesome bay colt. His coat glistened in the afternoon sun, and his neck was arched proudly as he pranced at the end of his lead line. He was on his toes, but he seemed to be in a good mood. Christina hoped he would act as good as he looked. Gratis snorted and tossed his head, dancing his rear end around, clearly eager to break free and run.

"In a few minutes, boy," Christina murmured to him. "Hang on just a little bit longer."

Without a word, Vince gave her a leg up, and in an instant she was on Gratis's back, automatically catching her stirrups with her toes. She wrapped the reins around her hands and waited for Vince's instructions.

Vince gazed up at Christina. "Just do your best, kid," he said. Then he released Gratis's head and patted the toe of her boot.

It was an odd form of encouragement, but Christina would take anything she could get. "I will," she promised.

As the groom led them off, Christina began to follow the movement of the horse beneath her.

Her heart thudded in her chest, and she felt Gratis dance nervously beneath her. "It's okay," she said softly, petting his neck. "I'm right here, boy. We'll be fine."

Gratis flicked his ears back at the sound of her voice, and Christina felt his tension ease a little.

Ahead of her she could see Star prancing at the end of his lead. She could see the whites of his eyes as he twisted away from Dani, trying to turn around. Christina's heart sank, but there was nothing she could do for Star. She had to trust that Melanie would take care of her precious colt.

"We're going to be all right, boy," she said to Gratis, stroking his neck. "I won't let you down, I promise."

"Good luck," the groom said as she handed the bay colt to the escort rider.

Christina could see Star ahead of Steve and Firefly as they paraded in front of the grandstand. To her relief, he seemed to be settling down, dancing a little beside the pony horse, but it looked to Christina that it was more excitement over the race than acting up. Star would be all right. She needed to focus on Gratis.

Christina rose in the saddle as they broke into a canter in front of the grandstand. Christina could feel the crowd watching them pass. Gratis felt calm and attentive. Christina hoped it would last until they were in the gate. "You're going to be awesome today," she said, feeling the power in Gratis's rippling muscles.

But as they neared the gate, Gratis pressed his ears back—the telltale sign that he planned to act up. She tightened up on the reins to distract him, but the pony rider had a good grip on his head.

"Can you loosen up on his head a little?" Christina asked the girl on the pony horse.

"Are you nuts?" The rider shook her head hard. "I've heard this horse is a real wacko. I'm not going to let him climb all over me!"

Christina could feel Gratis start to pick up his gait, tugging at the pony rider's grip. "He gets upset when he's held so tightly," she said. "Please, just give him a little room."

For a second Christina thought the girl was going to refuse, but then she let the lead shank out a couple of inches. Gratis seemed to relax a little, and Christina exhaled a heartfelt sigh of relief when they made it to the back of the starting gate.

She watched Star load easily, then waited as Steve and Dragonfly were shut into their slot in the staring gate.

As Gratis was led toward the chute, he began to prance, throwing his head up. Christina felt his front feet leave the ground, and she leaned forward on his shoulders.

"Come on, boy," she said. "It's okay. We'll be fine."

The colt dropped to the ground again, and Christina petted his neck. "A few steps and we'll be in, Gratis," she said.

"Give it up now, Reese," Steve called from the gate. "You're going to screw up the race for the rest of us."

"Shut up, Steve," Melanie yelled. "Just because you couldn't handle him doesn't mean my cousin can't. She's a great jockey."

"Whatever," Steve replied.

The crew got Gratis in front of the gate, then he lunged forward into his chute. He trembled a little as the gate clanged shut behind them. Christina patted the colt's neck gratefully.

"Good luck, Chris," she heard Melanie call.

"You and Star, too," she called back. "One back!" she heard the gate crew call.

She settled into a crouch on Gratis's back, preparing herself for the leaping start when the gate flew open.

As she took a deep breath, the starting bell echoed through her head. At the same instant the gate banged open. They were off!

CHRISTINA HAD A QUICK VIEW OF THE TRACK STRETCHING out ahead of them. Then Gratis made a magnificent bound from the gate, and they surged onto the track with the rest of the field. Gratis shot across the starting line, dropping over to the rail with the leaders. They had made it out of the gate! To her left Christina caught a quick glimpse of Melanie on Star, but she knew she had to focus on Gratis and let Melanie and Star run their own race.

As they closed on the first furlong, Christina's head was filled with the sounds of hooves thundering on the ground, the loud breathing of the racing horses, and the roar of the crowd. Over it all, the announcer's voice rang from the loudspeakers. "It's Like the Wind, number two, taking an early lead, with number one, Unconditional, at the rail, neck and neck with the number eight horse, Sunny Gold."

Ahead of her Christina could see the two horses who were fighting for second place, and in front of them, the rear of the chestnut, Like the Wind, who was in first. She could see Tommy Turner on Sunny Gold, holding second place next to Unconditional.

Gratis fought her hold, struggling to break loose and run wild. Christina could feel his frustration at being stuck behind the other horses. It took every bit of strength she had to keep him from running over the two horses directly in front of them.

Christina gritted her teeth and tightened her grip on the reins. She hoped she'd be able to keep Gratis under control throughout the race, but the colt wasn't making it easy.

She darted a look to her right, hoping for a chance to go wide, but Rockafella, a big gray who had drawn the number nine position, was fighting to get ahead of Gratis and move over to the rail. Christina urged Gratis to speed up a little, keeping the gray from cutting them off.

She peeked to the left and saw Steve Quinn's bay colt, Dragonfly, ducking closer to the rail, cutting Star and Melanie off.

"And it's Sunny Gold fighting Like the Wind for first," the announcer called, "with Unconditional falling back." As the number one horse slowed, Gratis was trapped, caught in the midst of the pack, and Christina could still see no chance of breaking free.

"As they come around the first turn," the announcer rang out, "it's Sunny Gold, Like the Wind, and Unconditional, with Dragonfly and Gratis close behind, and the rest of the field trailing."

Christina resisted glancing back to see where Star was compared to the rest of the field. She had to concentrate on Gratis. Ahead of her she could see Unconditional struggling. A tiny gap appeared between the number one and number two horses, and she pushed Gratis forward until they were side by side with Unconditional. As they came into the back stretch the brown number one horse looked as though he didn't have much left. But just when she moved toward the opening between Like the Wind and the rail, Steve pushed Dragonfly into the hole, blocking her maneuver. Christina glanced over at the jockey, seeing a look of grim determination on his face.

"Gratis is stuck behind Sunny Gold and Like the Wind, and Wonder's Star is at the rail behind Dragonfly, trying to find an opening. Now Like the Wind is dropping back as they come down the back stretch.

Sunny Gold is in the lead and moving onto the rail, with Gratis and Dragonfly coming up rapidly."

Christina leaned onto Gratis's shoulders, searching for a new opening as they thundered into the second turn. She could tell Gratis hadn't tapped into his speed yet. The colt had plenty more to give, if only she could give him the chance to do it.

"Now Rockafella is making a move." The announcer's voice carried across the infield. "The gray colt is coming up on the outside, boxing Gratis in behind Sunny Gold!" Christina felt Gratis tense, and she gritted her teeth. Right then it didn't matter if Gratis was the fastest horse in the world—as long as the more experienced jockeys were outmaneuvering her, he didn't have a ghost of a chance. She had to get Gratis out of the traffic and let him open up and run!

Then Dragonfly surged forward. As they came out of the turn, Steve and Dragonfly moved up on Sunny Gold, and Gratis was left holding third.

Beneath her, the colt was fighting to move out, but with Rockafella still to her right and Like the Wind between her and the rail, she was stuck behind Sunny Gold and Dragonfly. She tried to slow Gratis, giving him a shot at moving around Rockafella, but the colt refused to drop his speed, driving himself forward until his nose was almost in Dragonfly's tail.

She realized Like the Wind was dropping back, and she had just started to move toward the rail when the announcer's voice reached her over the raspy sound of the horses' labored breathing.

"Now Wonder's Star is passing Like the Wind and moving onto the rail. This is an exciting race! The fractions are amazing!"

Christina hesitated for a split second. Star was trying to squeeze onto the rail. The move she'd planned would block him! But she couldn't sacrifice the race for him; it wouldn't be right. She gritted her teeth and drove Gratis into the opening left by Like the Wind, cutting Star off.

As they pounded down the final stretch, a tiny gap opened between Dragonfly and the rail. Christina took a deep breath and pushed Gratis through.

"Now it's Gratis and Dragonfly, neck and neck, with Sunny Gold holding the lead as they come into the last stretch of the race!"

When he saw the open track in front of him, Gratis surged forward, exploding past Steve and Dragonfly. Christina glanced to her right to see a look of surprise on the other jockey's face as they swept past him.

Then they were bearing down on Sunny Gold.

She urged Gratis on with her hands and voice, and

he drew up alongside Sunny Gold as they flew down the straight stretch. She caught a glimpse of Tommy's face. The jockey was focused on the track in front of him, flicking his crop past Sunny's eye, and his colt rallied to find another gear.

Christina kneaded her hands up Gratis's neck, leaning into his shoulders. She balanced on her toes, keeping her weight forward. "Go!" she yelled at him. "Come on, Gratis!"

"It's Sunny Gold in the lead," the announcer's voice carried over the track, "with Gratis moving up on the rail, Dragonfly to the outside, and Wonder's Star looking for an opening as they come into the final seconds. This is an amazing race!"

Christina rocked forward, tangling her fingers in Gratis's mane. "Come on, boy, you can do this!" she called. In response, Gratis flipped his ears up. Christina could feel him change gears, moving faster than she had thought possible. "Gratis is moving ahead," the announcer said. "Sunny Gold is fighting to hold the lead, but Gratis is moving like a bullet!"

Christina could feel Gratis pouring everything he had into the final stretch.

"Sunny Gold is not giving up the rail, and Gratis is going wide and moving up on the number eight horse. But Wonder's Star is making his move now. He is passing Dragonfly and moving up on Gratis."

Christina leaned once more onto Gratis's shoulders, doing her best to keep from inhibiting his movements. "Come on, Gratis," she cried, balancing as lightly as she could on the tips of her toes and on her knuckles. "We can do this! Go!"

At the sound of her voice, Gratis dug in and put on an extra burst of speed. They shot past Tommy and Sunny Gold.

The announcer's voice rose with excitement. "It looks like Gratis as we come down to the wire. But here comes Wonder's Star, pouring it on!"

Christina could hear the roar of the crowd and, blended with that, the excited voice of the announcer blaring from the speakers. But the drumming hooves, the wind rushing past her ears, and the thundering of her own heart drowned out what he was saying. As they continued the fight to the wire, Gratis reached out, lengthening his strides as they neared the finish line.

They had done it! Gratis had won the Futurity! With just a few more strides to go, Christina saw a flash of copper to her right, and suddenly Star shot by, making a brilliant dash for the finish line. She flicked her crop past Gratis's eye, and the colt gave one last surge of power.

But as they crossed the line, she heard the announcer's voice ringing over the labored breathing of the horses and her own pounding heart.

"It's Wonder's Star! Wonder's Star wins the Breeder's Futurity!"

14

THE CROWD ROARED, AND CHRISTINA STRUGGLED TO BRING Gratis to a stop, watching Melanie circling Star ahead of her. For a split second a wave of disappointment swept over Christina. She and Gratis had been so close to winning. Then the reality settled over her. Star had won! Her colt had beaten the field, coming from behind to win the Breeder's Futurity!

She finally got Gratis stopped, and she jumped from his back as Melanie walked past her, leading Star.

"Way to go, Mel!" she exclaimed.

Melanie grinned broadly. "We won," she said happily, a look of amazement on her face. "We did it, Chris!"

Christina glanced around, scanning the crowd at the rail for familiar faces. She saw her parents heading for the winner's circle, and saw Parker and Kevin leaning against the rail, wide smiles on both their faces.

Vince Jones was striding onto the track, and Christina's happiness over Star's win faded. The trainer was glowering as he marched onto the track. Silently Christina handed him Gratis's reins.

"I'll talk to you in a minute," he said, then walked the colt away. Christina eyed his departing back, trying not to let his abruptness bother her. But as she walked off the track, a sense of gloom settled over her. Vince had every right to be upset with her. She'd lost the race.

Fredericka was by the rail, waiting for her. "You did a magnificent job," Gratis's owner said delightedly. "I'm so proud of both of you."

"Thanks," Christina replied, glancing around for Vince. If he was going to lecture her, she wanted to get it over with. She spotted the trainer, who was handing Gratis off to his groom. Then he headed back toward her, a serious look on his face. Christina stared up at him, her heart sinking rapidly.

"That was incredible," Vince said, still glowering.

Christina was confused. Vince didn't sound angry, he sounded . . . *proud*. "But I let you down!" she exclaimed in shock.

The trainer shook his head and smiled. It was the

first time Christina had ever seen him smile. "I was beginning to think Gratis would never get out of the gate in another race," he said. "You showed me what he can do. I might just start gearing him toward the Derby qualifying races. Are you interested in riding him again?"

Christina glanced over her shoulder to where Star was being led into the winner's circle. "I'd love to," she said, beaming. "That is, if I'm not riding Star."

"You have a brilliant future ahead of you, Christina," Vince said earnestly. "Both you and that cousin of yours."

"Thank you," Christina said, a warm glow coursing through her at the trainer's words of praise.

"Chris, come on!" she heard Melanie call. "Family photo in the winner's circle!"

"Enjoy yourself," Vince said and walked away.

Melanie's joy was infectious. Christina smiled at her cousin's radiant face. "You go on," she said, hugging Melanie. "You and Star deserve all the attention. You were amazing."

"Are you sure?" Melanie said, her eyes drifting to the circle, where Dani and Ashleigh were waiting with Star.

Christina nodded firmly. This was Melanie's moment in the spotlight. "We'll celebrate later, don't worry," she said with a laugh, and shoved Melanie toward the flashing cameras and applause waiting for her in the winner's circle.

"Chris!"

She wheeled around to see Parker pushing his way through the throng of people crowding near the winner's circle.

"That was great!" he said, wrapping his arms around her.

Christina gave him a hug. "Thanks for coming up to watch us," she murmured. "And thanks for getting Kevin to come up, too. I think it meant a lot to Mel."

The fans pressed around them, and Christina craned her neck to sneak a peek at the winner's circle. "Melanie and Star were pretty awesome, weren't they?" Christina said. "I couldn't believe it when Star shot right by us!"

Parker grinned. "You and Gratis put on a pretty good show yourselves. I don't know who was yelling louder, me or Kevin."

"Kevin? But he and Mel . . ."

"They'll get things worked out," Parker answered. "We thought we could have a little celebration at the Jockey Club later. How does that sound?"

"Like fun," Christina said. "But what about Mel and Kevin? Maybe they won't—"

"Look," Parker said, pointing toward the winner's circle.

Melanie was stepping off the scale, her saddle draped over her arm. She handed the saddle to Dani, and as the groom started to put it onto Star's back again, Kevin leaned over the rail. Melanie stepped over to him.

To Christina's delight, the pair hugged, and when Melanie turned back to Star, she was smiling happily. Then Ashleigh boosted her up on Star's back, and the cameras started snapping. Reporters leaned into the circle, calling questions. Melanie looked as though she was eating it up.

"Your mom and dad are going to have a tough time deciding who to put on their horses, you or Melanie," Parker said, chuckling.

"I know," Christina said proudly. "Whitebrook's pretty lucky to have two awesome jockeys like us."

MARY NEWHALL ANDERSON spent her childhood exploring back roads and trails on horseback with her best friend. She now lives with her husband, horse-crazy daughter Danielle, and five horses on Washington State's Olympic Peninsula. Mary has published novels and short stories for both adults and young adults.

Collect all the books in the Thoroughbred series

THOROUGHBRED Super Editions

ASHLEIGH'S Thoroughbred Collection

* coming soon

Which horse will Christina choose?

Star was in the race, and they had drawn an excellent starting position. She imagined them in the gate, waiting for the starting bell. She could feel the colt shifting beneath her, eager to run.

"This is going to be a great race," she murmured to Ashleigh, who looked pleased about Star's luck in the draw.

Ashleigh nodded. "You have a good gate position, and I know Star is in prime condition for this race. Now be quiet so we can hear which horses are going to fill the field."

The assistant's voice rang out again. "Dragonfly, Steve Quinn riding."

"Gate four," the secretary announced.

Christina winced. Steve would be beside her. She'd just have to deal with it, she decided. She wouldn't let him bother her.

Then the assistant held up another piece of paper. "Gratis," he said loudly. "Christina Reese riding."

"Number five," the secretary said, but Christina barely heard the colt's position number.

Her mind reeled. She didn't hear the last two positions being called as the assistant's words echoed in her head. Star and Gratis were in the same race—and she'd been named to ride both of them!